ESPECIALLY
MEDIA

CANDY HARPER

SIMON & SCHUSTER

First published in Great Britain in 2016 by Simon & Schuster UK Ltd
A CBS COMPANY

1 3 5 7 9 10 8 6 4 2

Simon & Schuster UK Ltd
1st Floor, 222 Gray's Inn Road
London
WC1X 8HB

www.simonandschuster.co.uk

Simon & Schuster Australia, Sydney
Simon & Schuster India, New Delhi

A CIP catalogue record for this book
is available from the British Library.

PB ISBN 978-1-4711-4708-1
eBook ISBN 978-1-4711-4709-8

Typeset in Bembo by M Rules
Printed and bound by CPI Group (UK) Ltd, Croydon, CR0 4YY

For my moody big sister, Naomi
(who grew up to be a real sweetheart)

CHAPTER ✤ ONE

You can never find a hairbrush in our house. You'd think that with four sisters and one mum, all with long hair, there would be plenty of combs and brushes and cute hairslides lying about, but the truth is that hairbrushes disappear quicker than chocolate-chip cookies in this place. Which is why I keep a secret supply in my bedroom. Of both cookies and a brush. But someone (and I had a pretty good idea of which someone) had stolen my secret brush.

I knew it wasn't Mum. She doesn't borrow my things. Chloe, who I share a bedroom with, is always taking my possessions without asking. But I ruled her out because even though she is only a year younger than me and therefore practically a teenager – meaning she should really start paying some attention to her appearance – she never brushes her hair if she can help it and, last time I saw Chloe, her hair was in its usual sticking-up-like-a-loo-brush state. My next sister down, Ella, is always neat and tidy, but her manners are far too good to go through my stuff. So that left my little sister, Lucy.

'Lucy!' I shouted. 'Where's my hairbrush?'

'It's twenty to twenty!' she shouted back. When Lucy doesn't want to answer your questions, she pretends that you asked her what the time is. Except she's only seven and she doesn't know how to tell the time, so it's always twenty to twenty in Lucy Land.

'I said, *where's my hairbrush?*' I shouted even louder.

No answer. I was supposed to be meeting my best friend, Lauren, to go shopping in town. Obviously, I couldn't shop with scrumpled hair. I stomped downstairs.

Lucy was in the sitting room surrounded by stuffed animals.

'Have you got my hairbrush?'

'I'm playing with my pets.'

I looked down at a toy hedgehog family who seemed to be about to attack a toy rabbit family with teaspoons. Then I spotted my hairbrush at the back of the line of hedgehogs. I picked it up.

2

'Don't take him!' Lucy shrieked.

And she actually snatched the brush back from me and whacked me on the arm with it.

'Ow! Don't smack me!'

'That's what you get for trying to tear a poor baby hedgehog away from its mother.'

I thought it was weird that Lucy would want a hairbrush; she's not exactly keen on keeping tidy. She'd obviously borrowed my hairbrush to complete her hedgehog family. Unbelievable.

'It's not a toy!' I said, grabbing it back. 'I need it to brush my hair.'

Lucy pushed past me and picked up the phone.

'What are you doing?'

'I'm going to call the RSPCA and tell on you.'

I rolled my eyes. 'Tell them what? That my hair is tangled? I haven't been cruel to any animals.' I waved the brush at her. 'This isn't actually a hedgehog.'

She hugged her largest cuddly hedgehog to her chest. 'But Prickles is and you've broken her heart.'

'Prickles is a stuffed toy!'

'*Shh!* You're hurting her feelings.'

I wrestled the phone out of her hand and slammed it back in place.

'I'll use Chloe's mobile,' she said.

'You don't even know the number for the RSPCA.'

3

'Yes I do. I learnt it off by heart from that sticker Mum used to cover up that chip in the car window.' She scowled at me. 'And I know the number for when it's cruelty to children and that's what you're doing. I'm going to phone them and then they'll come and take you away.'

'Good! Then maybe I can live somewhere nice and quiet without a load of annoying sisters!'

But Lucy didn't hear me because she'd already run out of the room, slamming the door behind her.

Honestly! This is the kind of madness I have to put up with.

I took a deep breath and started running the brush through my hair. I'm lucky that my hair isn't wiry like Chloe's or fluffy like Ella's. Mine is dead straight and shiny.

Before I'd finished my phone chirped and I slid it out of my pocket to see who was texting me. It was Lauren. At least my best friend never annoys me. She's brilliant, unlike my family; she completely gets me. Her texts always cheer me up.

Except this one didn't. It said: *Can't make it for shopping. I'm sick! Sorry. Call you later.*

I blew out a big breath. I hadn't seen Lauren all half-term because she'd been at her aunt's and now she was ill.

I thought about going shopping by myself, but it

4

isn't quite the same when you haven't got anyone to try outfits on with or make sarcastic remarks about how pouty the assistants in Topshop are. And I'd been sort of hoping that we might see Cute Josh from school. Sometimes he and his friends hang out in front of the skate shop. But I didn't feel like trying to spot him without Lauren.

I thought about asking Chloe if she wanted to go into town. When we were little, Chloe and I were good friends, then, a year and a half ago, our parents got divorced and everything changed. I thought that the break-up was completely my dad's fault and I got really cross with him, and with Chloe, because I thought that she was taking his side.

Recently, my mum has explained things to me and now I understand that my parents got divorced because that was what they both wanted to do. And I realised it was stupid for me to be mad at Chloe because she wasn't taking sides and, despite the fact she's a bit sweaty and noisy, she's actually quite a good sister. But, even though we've spent most of this half-term moving things around so that Chloe and I are sharing a bedroom again, we still don't exactly have a lot of interests in common. When I go shopping, I like looking at clothes and the market stall with all the gothic jewellery, whereas Chloe likes JD Sports and the bakery. Anyway, she was in the garden with her giant friend, Thunder. They were supposed to be playing badminton, except I think that in the official rules players don't whack each other with the rackets quite so much.

I went looking for Ella; she's only eleven, but she's quite sensible really and she's the kind of person who does stuff when you ask her to.

'Ella, do you want to go into town with me?' I said, sticking my head into the room that she shares with Lucy.

Ella looked up. She was crouched over on the floor surrounded by squares of card and coloured pencils.

'Um . . .' she said. 'I'm making revision cards for maths. We've got a test next week and Ashandra's coming over to revise with me tomorrow, but I could finish them later.'

I hesitated. Last week, my dad came to watch me sing at the International Day at school and we ended up having a big chat about the divorce. It started me thinking about my behaviour since my parents split up. I've decided that I don't want to be such a negative person. I've also realised that maybe sometimes, just sometimes, I can be a tiny bit, well, selfish, and I want to change that too. So I said to Ella, 'It's fine. I might not bother with town. Go on making your cards.'

She tried to hide it, but she was obviously relieved I wasn't dragging her away. Then her face clouded. 'Do you think revision cards are silly?' she asked.

I certainly never put that much effort into a little test.

'I don't think they're silly,' I said. 'Super boring, but not silly.'

I have also been thinking about giving up saying mean things.

I'm not quite there yet.

Ella didn't seem to mind though. She's used to me. She went back to writing numbers in different colours and I sloped downstairs to where Lucy's rabbits were being massacred by the spoon-wielding hedgehogs. I've always thought of hedgehogs as being quiet animals, but these ones were managing some blood-curdling battle cries.

I sat down on the sofa and put my head in my hands. Now what was I supposed to do? It was the second to last day of half-term and the only people I had to hang out with were loopy Lucy and her vicious animal friends.

CHAPTER ♥ TWO

I don't like the second half of the autumn term. It's always raining and cold and my mum constantly tells us to put hats on. Hats are the enemy of smooth hair. And if you've got a long face, like I have, once you put a hat on top it's hard to avoid looking like a mushroom.

Our second day back at school after half-term started with freezing sleet and Mum went on about not getting chilly heads, plus Lauren was still ill so I had to sit by myself in half my lessons for the second day running. All in all, I wasn't in a very good mood by the time Chloe, Ella and I got home from school and peeled off our sopping coats and evil mushroom hats. Ella, on the other hand, practically skipped upstairs to change her wet tights and Chloe was so cheerful that she was actually dancing round the kitchen while she made a sandwich.

'What have you got to be so happy about?' I asked.

She beamed at me. 'Something amazing has happened.'

When Chloe says something amazing has happened, it's normally about the number of burps she has managed to do after drinking a family-sized bottle of Coke really fast.

I frowned. I mean, I was already frowning, but I tightened my forehead even more. 'Is it about burping?'

'Nope,' Chloe said.

'Farting?'

'Well, I did do one in the bath last night that sounded like someone revving an underwater motorbike, but actually it's about rugby.'

I sighed. 'I think it's just possible that rugby is the one thing I find less interesting than your bodily functions.'

'But this is brilliant. Thunder's uncle's friend's cousin plays for the Chiefs and, guess what?' Chloe didn't wait for me to ask what or even give me an opportunity to block my ears to avoid hearing whatever dull rambling was coming next. 'They're starting a youth squad! They're going to do trials and someone is coming into our school to talk about it.'

'Oh, that's just super,' I said.

'I know.'

The thing about being sarcastic is that it doesn't really work if the other person is too busy licking peanut butter straight from the jar to notice.

I looked at Chloe. Her eyes were shining. She really does love rugby. Since I was trying to be a bit kinder to my family instead of always pointing out how ridiculous they are, I swallowed all my hilarious jokes about rugby and said, 'I hope you get on the squad.'

She grinned back at me. 'I will.'

Chloe and Ella were in such good moods that we had a pretty peaceful time eating snacks and chatting until Mum came home with Lucy. Even though Lucy finishes school before us, she has to stay at After School Club until Mum picks her up. As soon as Lucy got in the door, the quiet, chilled atmosphere disappeared.

'Urgh!' Lucy stomped into the sitting room where Ella and I were watching TV, shaking herself like a dog so that raindrops flew off her red-gold curls and landed on the carpet. She threw herself down on the sofa, narrowly avoiding knocking my cup of tea out of my hands.

'Hey!' I said. 'If you spill my tea, you'll have to make me a new cup.'

'I am not allowed to use the kettle,' she snapped back. 'And when I'm big enough to use it I'll make you a cup of tea and I'll spit in it.'

'That's enough of that, young lady,' Mum said, coming in and putting her laptop on the table.

'What's the matter, Lucy?' Ella asked.

Lucy stuck out her bottom lip. 'Everyone is horrible.'

'Have you only just worked that out now?' I asked.

'Just because you've had a tiff at school doesn't mean everyone is horrible,' Mum said, shooting me a look. 'You've got a lovely family.'

Lucy opened her mouth to disagree so Mum quickly went on, 'And you've got lots of nice friends.'

'Hmpf!' Lucy smashed her fist into a cushion.

'Have you fallen out with someone?' Ella asked.

'I didn't *fall* out,' Lucy sniffed. 'I *jumped* out and away from her because that's what you should do when someone is horrible to you.'

'I don't think she meant to be horrible,' Mum said.

'Who are you talking about?' Ella asked.

'Emily.'

11

I turned back to the TV. Lucy's battles with her friends are long and complicated and I get confused because sometimes they're intermixed with the battles that go on in her fantasy land of rainbow ponies and robo-giants. Although it's pretty obvious to me that Lucy's friends are more scared of her than they are of the robo-giants.

'Which Emily?' Ella asked. 'There are two in your class.'

'Evil Emily.'

I snorted. 'I thought they were called Tall Emily and Little Emily. Which one is it?'

Lucy folded her arms. 'Little Emily, but she's more evil than she is little.'

'Why is she evil?' Ella asked.

'Today we had to put up our hands to vote for who should be library monitor and she didn't put up her hand for me.' Lucy glared with hard eyes, waiting for us to be horrified.

Nobody was horrified.

'Shocking,' I said.

'Yes it is,' Lucy pouted.

I'm going to have to make my family watch a video about sarcasm so they can understand when I'm doing it.

'People put their hands up for Ella yesterday,' Lucy explained.

Ella looked up from laying out her school books on the table. She likes to get her homework done as soon as possible. Sometimes I worry she might try to do it on the way home from school and bump into a bus.

'What's Lucy talking about, Ella?' Mum asked. 'Were you in a vote yesterday?'

Ella wriggled in her chair. 'Yes.'

I rolled my eyes. Ella could be nominated for president of the world and she would keep it quiet. 'Come on then,' I said. 'Tell us what it was for.'

'Tutor group captain.'

'Did you get many votes?'

Ella was as pink as her heart-shaped rubber by now. 'Quite a lot. Actually, I won.'

Crazy. When I win something, I like to tell everyone. That way I get to feel winnerish for even longer. Sometimes I don't understand Ella at all.

'That's great!' Mum said. 'Well done, Ella. I'm really proud of you.'

'Yeah, good one,' I said, but I couldn't help adding, 'even though you're a traitor for becoming a cog in the hate machine of school that will crush us all in the end.'

Ella beamed. She doesn't think school is a hate machine. No wonder I don't understand her.

'Stop talking about Ella!' Lucy snapped. 'I started this talking; it's supposed to be about me.'

'But you haven't even been voted for,' I said.

'Exactly! That's what I'm talking about. It's stupid that they didn't vote for me. I'm really good at things. Ella isn't. You can hardly even hear Ella.'

Mum gave Lucy a sharp look. 'That's not a bad thing. We never stop hearing you.'

Lucy looked genuinely shocked. 'That's because I've got a lot of important things to say!'

Mum took hold of her hand. '*I've* got something important to say so listen hard: you can't make people vote for you. You have to let them choose whoever they think is the right person and if that isn't you then it's no good getting cross with them because that will make them even less likely to vote for you in future. Try being kind to your friends and I'm sure you'll get picked for something one day.'

Mum clearly thought that was the end of the matter and she went off to make our tea, but Lucy carried on moaning and groaning until it was time to eat. Then she went suspiciously quiet and I knew that she was plotting something. Mum can say what she likes about Lucy needing to treat her friends kindly, but I remember the last time Lucy fell out with one of them: there were lots of tears, a number of hidden lunch boxes and one very traumatised pet goldfish.

Later on, when I was doing the washing-up with Mum, I realised that in all the Lucy dramatics no one had shown any interest in Mum's day. Out of everyone in my family, my mum particularly deserves me being a bit more considerate; she's always thinking of other people.

'How was your day?' I asked her.

'Oh, you know, lots of noisy children. I always enjoy hearing what they've been up to over their holidays.'

'Really?' I pulled a face. I don't know how Mum can bear teaching Year Twos all day. 'Surely they do the same thing at home as they do at school: run around in circles, shouting.'

Mum laughed. 'They do all sorts. Georgia told me today that she helped her mum clear up "all the feathers", then I found out that the feathers had come out of a cushion Georgia was using to "sledge" down the stairs.'

I crossed my eyes. I'd been feeling sorry for myself because Lauren wasn't at school, but at least I didn't have to rely on seven-year-olds for entertainment.

Mum handed me a plate to dry. 'Then we did Picasso-style painting this afternoon; that's always nice. Even Shane Bolton can do that and it's so important to catch Shane doing something well occasionally.'

She smiled at me, but I thought it looked a bit like one of those smiles that I have to do when I open presents from Granny so I said, 'Are you sure you're all right? You seem a bit . . .' I'm not always very good at telling how other people are feeling so I tried, 'stressed?'

'Not stressed; in fact, for once, I feel like I'm on top of everything work-wise. I just . . .' She trailed off.

'Just what?'

Mum rinsed out the dishcloth. 'I've been thinking that maybe it would be nice to have something other than work to occupy me.'

'What sort of thing?'

'Oh, I don't know. Maybe I should take an evening class.'

I can't think why anyone would want to do any more lessons than they absolutely have to, but I know that my mum works really hard and I'm always telling her she should do more fun stuff. 'That's a good idea. I could babysit,' I offered.

Mum laughed.

'What? I already look after Chloe and Ella when we come home from school until you get back.'

'That's different. It's only for an hour and Lucy's not there.'

It's true that the best people to look after Lucy would be two bouncers and a lion tamer, but I was pretty sure that I could manage. I chewed my lip. I was trying hard to be helpful and Mum didn't even seem to want my help.

'You're always saying that I should be more responsible,' I said. 'This would be an excellent way to show you that I can be.'

Mum looked sceptical. 'I'm not sure you're quite mature enough yet, sweetheart.'

'But I want to do it!' I said. Then I realised that that probably didn't sound very mature. 'I mean, I'd really like you to be able to go to an evening class.'

Mum patted my hand. 'That's very thoughtful. But I could always choose a class on a Wednesday night; that way you girls would be at your dad's and we wouldn't need a babysitter. Maybe I'll pick up a prospectus from the learning centre.'

Ella spent the evening with her coloured pens and a lot of Post-it notes. I guessed she was taking her new role as tutor group captain seriously; they were going to be super organised from now on. Chloe was busy messaging people about the exciting opportunity to run around getting muddy while chasing a funny-shaped ball. I wanted to speak to Lauren about our chances of getting another solo in the carol concert this year. Last year, we were the only people chosen from Year Eight and it was amazing. We had to go to all these special rehearsals with the older soloists and even the singers from Years Twelve and Thirteen started saying hello to us when they saw us around school. The best thing was that our music teacher, Mr Garcia, gave us individual tuition and I know that my singing improved loads.

But when I rang Lauren to chat about it she didn't answer. Or call me back. Which was weird because normally, even if she's busy when I ring, she gets back to me really soon. Or at least she used to; when I thought about it, I realised that, over the last two weeks, I hadn't spoken to Lauren as much as I usually do. I wondered about going round to see her, but it was getting late.

When I went to bed, as I walked past Lucy and Ella's bedroom, I could see a lump under Lucy's duvet and the faint light of a torch glowing beneath the covers. Before she'd been sent to bed by Mum, I'd heard Ella trying to advise Lucy to be less bossy with her friends, but Lucy interrupted her to say that she could sort her own friends out, and I was pretty sure that now she was working on some terrible scheme to get back at them.

It seemed like everyone had big ideas about what they were going to do at school this term. If only Lauren would hurry up and get better then we could get on with our own brilliant plans.

CHAPTER ❦ THREE

The next day, Lauren still wasn't back at school and I had to spend lunchtime with Milly and Jasveen, who are my next-best-friends after Lauren. Which is fine, except when they have their own private jokes. Normally, I don't care because when they start sniggering and wiggling their eyebrows, I look at Lauren and Lauren looks at me and we both know what we're thinking. Other people's private jokes are much more annoying when you haven't got anyone to agree with you about just how annoying they are.

Because it was Wednesday I couldn't even pop round to see Lauren; on Wednesday nights, and every other weekend, we stay at our dad's house. When my parents first got divorced and I was mad at my dad, I found it hard to spend time with him and his girlfriend, Suvi. Then they had a baby, Kirsti, and I felt even crosser with both of them. I spent quite a long time being cross actually, but, since I've had that big chat with my mum, I know that my parents just didn't want to be married any more and it was nobody's fault. Not even Suvi's. And I do believe that. So, even though Suvi still isn't exactly my favourite person, I'm trying harder not to be mad at her. At least you always know where you stand with Suvi. She's always cool and calm. I used to call her the Ice Queen.

But today, when we arrived at Dad's house and Suvi opened the door, she didn't look at all like an ice queen. Her usually smooth white-blonde hair was tangled and her pale cheeks were flushed.

'Hello, girls. Did you all have a good day?' She wasn't actually looking at us when she said it, so I could tell she wasn't really interested, and I just said, 'Revolting', without going into details.

We all trooped into the kitchen. Ella got out her maths textbook and Chloe started rifling through the cutlery drawer.

'Is Kirsti awake yet?' Lucy asked, crawling out from under the table and making me jump. On Wednesdays, Lucy doesn't have to go to After School Club because Suvi is on maternity leave and she picks Lucy up from school at the normal finishing time.

21

Lucy loves it because she gets to spend as much time as possible with baby Kirsti. But she's not too keen on Kirsti sleeping. Lucy thinks people should be available to her twenty-four hours a day.

Suvi ran a hand across her face. 'Kirsti's still having her nap.'

'Can I wake her up?' Lucy asked.

'No!' Suvi never snaps, but that was the closest to snapping I'd ever heard her get. She put a hand on Lucy's arm. 'I promise you can play with her soon, Lucy, but Kirsti's not sleeping so well at night. I think she needs this nap now.'

'You seem tired,' Ella said to Suvi. 'Shall I make you a cup of peppermint tea?'

I looked at Suvi again. She was a bit red around the eyes. I hadn't noticed. It's funny how the kind of person you are affects what you can see. When Suvi first opened the door, I'd thought she looked like a woman who needed to brush her hair, but Ella saw someone who needed looking after. While Ella fussed over Suvi and got her to put her feet up in the sitting room with her cup of manky peppermint tea, and Lucy went to wait outside Kirsti's bedroom door, I plonked myself down beside Chloe, who was getting aggressive with a bunch of bananas.

'Why are you squashing those bananas with a potato masher?' I asked.

'Because it's quicker than a fork.'

'Yeah, but what are the bananas for?'

Chloe didn't stop mashing. 'I'll think of something.'

There's not much point talking to Chloe when she's in a bashing or smashing mood: it's best to move all your valuables to a safe distance and let her get on with it. So I put my phone on a high shelf and opened up the fridge to see if Suvi had anything to eat that hadn't had all the sugar and flavour squeezed out of it, but Chloe let out a gusty sigh and said, 'Aren't you even going to ask me about my day?'

'I asked you about your day when we were walking home from school. You said you didn't want to talk about it.'

'When someone says that, you're supposed to gently persuade them to tell you what's wrong.'

We looked at each other. Gentle persuasion is not my strong point.

'Oh, all right, I'll just tell you,' Chloe huffed. 'Something absolutely disgusting has happened.'

Now alarm bells were ringing in my brain because I know from experience that it takes a lot for Chloe to say that something is disgusting. When we found a dead seagull in the garden that had started to decompose, Chloe said it was 'cool'.

So it had to be something pretty rank for Chloe to say it was disgusting. I was going to tell Chloe that, thanks to her, I had enough revolting images in my mind to last me a lifetime, but then I noticed that she was gripping the masher so hard that her knuckles were white. So I gave in and said, 'What's happened?'

'That man came into school today to talk about the rugby youth squad.'

'Is that all? Well, physical exercise *is* fairly disgusting, but I thought you liked all that running about and sweating? You've certainly got the legs to be a rugby player. And the ears.'

'Thanks. But that's not it. They said ... they said ... you're not going to believe it ... they said that it's a *boys-only* squad.'

It's funny being a sister. Chloe is annoying and loud and smelly and I don't give a monkey's who's allowed on some silly squad, but I still found myself saying, 'That's so unfair!' And I really meant it.

'That's what I said.'

'And what did the man say?'

She switched the masher to her left hand and went on crushing the already pulpy bananas. 'He said that rugby was more of a boys' sport so they'd set the squad up specifically for them and didn't the school have a girls' team I could join?'

'Patronising pig!'

'That's what I said. Only I couldn't think of the word patronising so I just called him a pig.'

I laughed. 'Not to his face?'

'Not *exactly* to his face. I mean, he was still at the front of the sports hall with Mr Evans and everyone was shuffling about, getting ready to go to the next lesson, so he didn't hear me.'

'Good.'

'But Mrs Henderson did.'

'Oh.'

'So I had to spend my lunch break tidying the equipment cupboard.'

I shook my head. I can't stand Mrs Henderson; she's always shouting at me to get moving, or to stop standing in the middle of the field like a daydreaming daisy and chase after the ball, but you'd think she'd be more sympathetic to a sports freak like Chloe.

'I'm sorry, Clo, that's really rough. I don't know why they always put idiots in charge of things.'

She nodded grimly and peeled another banana.

Suvi perked up a bit after her tea and, by the time Dad came home from work, she'd got us all making banana bread with Chloe's thrashed bananas while Kirsti watched from her bouncy chair.

'Something smells good,' Dad said. He made his way across the kitchen, kissing everyone as he went. For a long time, I was so mad with him about the divorce and for how little time he was spending with us that I wouldn't let him hug or kiss me, but, after he apologised about all of that, things have been a lot better. He really has changed the way he acts. And I have a bit too. Part of me just wanted to be angry forever because I needed my parents, and Suvi, to know that I don't think it's fair on the kids when parents get divorced. But actually it's quite tiring being angry all the time and I sort of missed my dad, so I decided that I just have to be realistic about my parents: they live in different houses, but they're both still my parents and I can still ask them for help and chat to them and get annoyed with them and do all the normal stuff.

So these days I let Dad kiss me. As long as no one I know is watching.

Chloe flung her arms round Dad. She's never been cross with him. In fact, Chloe isn't usually cross with anyone. But this rugby thing must have really upset her because she started telling him the whole story right from the beginning. He listened carefully. Which is one of the good changes that he's made. Not long ago, whenever you were telling my dad something, he'd have one eye on his phone.

'That doesn't seem very fair,' he said when Chloe got to the end. 'Why don't you speak to your PE teacher about it?'

'Yes,' Suvi said. I hadn't realised that she was listening, but actually she was staring quite hard at Chloe. 'Yes,' she said again. 'You must speak to this teacher.'

Chloe shrugged. 'All right, I'll give it a go.'

CHAPTER ♦ FOUR

Our school is very proud of its music. We have two orchestras, four choirs, a jazz group, an African drumming club and free percussion lessons for anyone who can hold a beater. Mr Garcia, the head of music, is really clever and can play any instrument you can think of. He's even played the piano on some proper musicians' albums. He does wear horrible patterned jumpers though. Apart from that, I quite like him because he organises lots of music stuff for us to take part in.

Every year, before Christmas, we have a carol concert. Last year, I sang the first verse of 'In the Bleak Midwinter' as a solo. I like 'In the Bleak Midwinter' better than all those jingle-jangle carols. And if you'd ever had to share a bedroom with Chloe after she's eaten a plate of sprouts for lunch then you'd know that Christmas can be pretty bleak.

The first meeting about the carol concert was after school on Thursday. Lauren missed it because she still wasn't back at school, but I called her as soon as it finished.

'Hey, Amelia.' She sounded groggy. I think I might have woken her up.

'Hey, yourself. How are you? I haven't heard from you for days. Are you really rough?'

'I'm OK. It's just the flu or something. I was going to call you, but I've been sleeping loads.'

'Sorry you're so ropey.'

'Who are you calling ropey? I'm sorry you're so flaky.'

I laughed. I'd missed chatting to Lauren. 'I hope you get better soon,' I said.

'I will,' she said. 'What's happening at school?'

'Well, I've just been to the first meeting about the Christmas concert and guess what?' I said.

'What?'

'No cathedral this year.'

'Oh. Does that mean no concert?'

'Nope, but it does mean that things will be completely different.'

She made a sort of *huh* noise, which I took as encouragement to tell her everything I knew. 'Mr Garcia seems really excited about it. You know how he twitches when he's conducting? He was doing that just talking to us. I think he's sick of hymns and carols. So we're not doing any of them. Instead, it's going to be Christmas songs.'

'Carols are Christmas songs.' She still sounded half asleep.

'Yes, but we're not doing churchy ones; we're doing, you know, pop stuff.'

'Like what?'

'"All I Want for Christmas".'

'Sounds a bit cheesy.'

'He's chosen some good ones, honestly, and there are going to be solos and duets. I thought that you and me c—'

'Amelia? Sorry, my mum's calling. I'll phone you at the weekend, OK?'

And she hung up before I'd finished telling her my ideas about which solos we should try out for. I was a little bit hurt. Normally, Lauren is the one person who's happy to listen to me going on about singing and performing all day long. But she was ill and tired and her mum is one of those demanding mothers that expect you to actually pay attention to every tiny little thing they say. We'd be able to have a proper talk about the concert when Lauren came back to school.

'You walking home?' Milly called across the hall to me.

'Yep.'

'Come on then.'

I struggled into my coat and we walked out through the gates with the last few stragglers from rehearsal.

'It's a shame Lauren wasn't there,' Milly said. 'Do you think Mr Garcia will say she can't be in the concert now she's missed a rehearsal?'

Milly's my friend and I do like her, but she's got this habit of saying really provocative things. She loves stirring up trouble.

'Of course he won't. It's not her fault she's ill.'

'I suppose it'll be all right if she comes back soon. She was off a lot last half-term, wasn't she?'

'Not really,' I said, although now I thought about it Lauren had missed quite a few days. 'She had to go to Scotland for her cousin's wedding and then she had problems with her brace.'

Milly shrugged. 'I thought she might be getting glandular fever again.'

Lauren had glandular fever in the summer and she was off school for ages. I'd really missed her.

'You don't get it twice,' I said, even though I wasn't sure if that was true. 'Did you see Mr Garcia's face when that little Year Seven scraped his chair back when he was in the middle of explaining the harmonies?' I added, trying to change the subject.

I kept the conversation away from Lauren until it was time for us to go our separate ways. I watched Milly's back for a moment. I really hoped Lauren would get well quickly. I wanted her back at school so we could moan about teachers and enjoy the concert rehearsals together, like we always do.

CHAPTER ❦ FIVE

I was walking down the corridor to chemistry on Monday morning when Chloe grabbed my arm.

'What is it?' I asked. She was pink in the face and out of breath.

'It's Thunder. He went to those youth squad trials on Saturday and they've picked him for the team.'

I wasn't especially concerned about getting to chemistry on time so I stopped and pulled her to one side of the fast-moving flow of students.

She was scowling; I wondered if she'd pulled that face when Thunder told her.

'Did you congratulate him?' I asked.

'It's completely not fair. He's not even as good as me at rugby. Would you congratulate someone that got a singing part that you knew you'd be much better at?'

She had me there. 'No. But everybody knows that you're a nicer person than I am so people expect more from you.'

'Well, I don't feel very nice at the moment.'

'I'm sorry, Clo, but it's not Thunder's fault that they won't let you on the squad. It's not worth falling out over.' I suddenly felt like Mum when I said that. 'Anyway, aren't you supposed to be somewhere?'

'Aren't *you* supposed to be somewhere?'

'Yep, chemistry. Can't you see I'm rushing to get there?' I mimed an ultra-slow walk.

Chloe turned in the opposite direction and shuffled forward with tiny steps. 'I'm off to French. Running all the way.'

I laughed and Chloe managed a snort.

'I'm not happy though,' she called over her shoulder. 'Not happy at all.'

Which worried me a bit because Chloe is usually always happy.

Mum had a staff meeting that night so, by the time she'd picked up Lucy from her After School Club and brought her home, I had almost finished making spaghetti bolognese for our tea.

Mum was on her mobile when she came into the kitchen with Lucy and Chloe behind her.

'Lovely,' she said into her phone and mimed a kiss at me. 'I'll see you then. I'm looking forward to it. Bye now.'

She put her phone down and squeezed my shoulder. 'This looks fantastic,' she said.

'Who was that?' I asked.

She lifted five plates from the rack and handed them to Chloe to put on the table. 'Remember when I was talking about an evening class?'

'Uh-huh.'

'Well, I've decided to join a book club instead. That was the lady who organises it. My first meeting is on Wednesday.'

'A book club?' Lucy said. 'What's that? Do you all sit around reading? That doesn't sound very interesting. You can do reading in your own bed and nothing really happens. Except when Chloe climbs in and does a Dutch oven.'

'What on earth is a Dutch oven?' Mum asked.

'It's when you're in bed with someone and you pull the duvet over their head and then fart so that they're trapped with your stink,' Chloe said in a matter-of-fact way, as if this was a completely acceptable way to be talking when I was actually hoping to eat my tea without vomiting on my plate.

'You don't sit around reading at book clubs,' I said to Lucy. 'You read the book before you go and then, when you're there, you discuss the book and answer questions about it.'

'What on earth?' Chloe said. 'That's not a club! That's English lessons. Why would you want to do that, Mum?'

'I like reading books,' said Mum. 'And I thought it would be nice to meet some new people.'

'What's wrong with us?' Lucy demanded. 'I can talk to you about books any time you like.'

'There's nothing wrong with you, my sweet,' Mum said.

'Apart from the obvious,' I muttered.

'Nothing at all,' Mum said more loudly. 'But it's always good to make new friends, isn't it? Now, are we ready to eat, Amelia? Shall I call Ella?'

The bolognese was delicious (even if I do say so myself). But it was less enjoyable listening to Lucy telling us the plot of every book she's ever read (which fortunately isn't very many). I was grateful that I'd finished my tea by the time she got on to a story called *The Most Revolting Sandwich in the World*. I'm pretty sure she wrote that one herself.

CHAPTER ❤ SIX

The next day, Lauren finally came back to school. Even though she'd called me to say she was better, it was still almost a surprise to see her back in our tutor room. I tried to be cool and not get overexcited like a little kid, but I was so pleased to see her that I did say, 'You're here!' in quite a squealy way.

'I am!' Lauren said.

And then we hugged and I might have let out one more little squeal.

'How do you feel?' I asked. 'You're a bit pale.'

'You sound like my mum!'

'So you're over the flu?'

'Amelia, I'm completely fit and healthy.'

'OK, just checking.' I couldn't stop myself from grinning. 'This is brilliant!'

Lauren laughed. 'Yep. I've never seen you so excited about school.'

'I'm not excited about school. School is a miserable torture prison. I'm happy because you're here to share in it with me.'

'That's very moving,' Lauren said in a not-at-all-moved voice.

It was so good to be back with someone else who likes being sarcastic.

I punched her on the arm. 'I've got so much to tell you.'

She rubbed her arm. 'I know you're a bit thick and that violence is one of the few ways you can express yourself, but try to tell me the news without any more injuries, all right?'

I smirked. 'We'll see . . .'

'I need to hear more about the Christmas concert first.'

I made myself comfy on a chair. 'I told you we had the first meeting last week, and Mr Garcia gave out music and lyrics booklets, so I got one for you. I'll bring it in tomorrow. The rehearsals are on Thursdays, plus extra ones if you've got a solo.'

Olivia, who sits in front of us, dumped her bag on her chair and sat on the table. 'Are you talking about the concert?' she asked.

Lauren nodded. 'Sounds like it's going to be really good this year.'

Olivia sighed. 'I bet you two get solos.'

'I bet you do too,' Lauren said.

My mum says that when someone says a nice thing like that, you ought to say something nice back and it's called returning the compliment. But I think that's stupid if what you're saying isn't true. Not so long ago, I used to deliberately try and hurt people's feelings; now I've realised that that's pretty childish and unkind, but I still think it's ridiculous to say things that are obviously lies. We all know Olivia won't get a solo. But I'm trying not to upset people so I managed to give her a smile. It was supposed to be an encouraging smile, but I haven't given out many of those so I'm not sure how successful it was.

Then Mrs Bixby came in and we had to listen to the register.

I poked Lauren. 'Olivia's right about you; you'll definitely get a solo.'

She couldn't help smiling. The great thing about Lauren is that I never have to say any silly compliment things to her that aren't true. She really has got a brilliant voice. And she's smart. And funny. Sometimes my teachers and my parents go on at me about being nicer, but I'm nice to Lauren because it's really easy. She's basically a perfect friend. At least, she usually is; I felt like we'd been a bit out of touch while she was ill. But I knew that everything would get back to normal now she was better.

After registration, it was English. Music and drama are my favourite subjects, but English is quite bearable. I don't know why people ever say reading is boring. So much stuff happens in books. Terrible stuff. It's brilliant. Plus, no one ever tells people in books to stop being dramatic and go and lay the table.

I quite like our English teacher, Mrs Holt; she gets us to do a lot of group work because she says we'll understand a text better if we can have a good argument about it. I'm very good at arguing. The other great thing about English this year is that all the tutor groups have been mixed up and Cute Josh is in our class. He's in our maths and science lessons too.

'How have you been getting on with CJ?' Lauren asked in a low voice while we were settling into our seats in Mrs Holt's classroom. She used our code for Cute Josh so that no one knew who we were talking about. Lauren is the expert on Cute Josh; he knows her name because her mum and Josh's mum used to work together. Last year, he even came round to her house to pick up something for his mum. Back then, we hadn't realised just how cute

Cute Josh is; it was only after the summer holidays that we noticed him. He seemed to have grown about fifteen centimetres and he'd obviously been somewhere hot on holiday because he was really tanned and his hair was all blond and tousled like a surfer's.

In our first maths lesson, Mr Ireland got Josh to hand out the protractors and when I took one from the box he was holding out to me he said, 'Wait, that one's cracked,' and chose me a new one. So he's cute *and* nice.

'Nothing major to report,' I whispered back. 'But last week Mrs Holt made him read out loud so I got to listen to him for ages.'

'What was he like at reading?'

I laughed. 'He didn't seem to have any problems. Managed all the tricky words; didn't run his finger along the page or anything.'

'I meant, did he make it sound good, like a drama teacher, or is he one of those that hide behind the book?'

'I think he was a bit embarrassed to start with, but he is a good reader; everyone was listening.'

Lauren did a fake big sigh. 'I wonder what he sounds like reading love poetry,' she said in a silly high-pitched voice.

We cracked up. I was so glad she was finally back.

Even though we were sitting near Josh, he didn't say hello to Lauren, like he sometimes does, but he did answer two questions correctly, which is a good thing. I don't know why anyone fancies stupid people. I'm not interested in anyone who can't understand my jokes.

In drama, once we'd got into our groups, Milly started explaining everything to Lauren in quite an over-the-top, patronising way. 'It's all right,' Lauren said. 'They sent some books and stuff home. I've already read the play.'

I didn't know that the school had sent her work. They normally only do that when people get excluded and they don't come in for ages. Lauren had only been off for a week.

'We're doing the first scene,' Jasveen said. 'And then the other groups follow on from us.'

'Can I be the mother?' Lauren asked.

Milly opened her mouth to speak, but I got in first. 'We've sort of already worked out the parts, remember? I told you when I spoke to you at the weekend,' I said.

Lauren's forehead creased. She didn't look like she remembered at all. 'So who's the mother?'

'I am,' Milly said. 'And you're the maid.'

'OK,' Lauren said. But she didn't look very OK about it.

'We haven't done that much work on it,' I said. 'We could still swap around parts.'

Milly and Jasveen looked at each other.

'The thing is,' Milly said, 'the mother is the biggest part. It needs to be someone who is prepared to do a lot of rehearsing.'

'I am,' Lauren said. 'Completely committed.'

Milly rolled her eyes. 'But are you definitely going to be here? You've just had a whole week off and you missed loads of days before half-term too.'

'I'm here now,' Lauren said in a cold voice.

'Yeah, she's better now, aren't you, Lauren?'

Lauren didn't answer that; instead, she said, 'If you want the part so much, Milly, you can have it.' And she walked off to talk to Olivia and Bethany on the other side of the room.

'I was just saying,' Milly said. 'If we want it to be good, we all have to be here to practise.'

'Maybe Milly and Lauren could both learn the mother's part and the maid's part,' Jasveen said. 'Then we could see who does it best.'

Milly shrugged. 'I suppose we could do that. But whoever is playing the mother has to be here for absolutely every single lesson.'

'Lauren will be,' I said.

And I hoped it was true.

CHAPTER 🍓 SEVEN

The next day we were nearly late for school. Mum had been so busy reading the final few chapters of her book for the first book club meeting that night that she forgot to wake anybody up. When we finally scrambled out of bed, it was chaos while we all dashed about. Lucy and Chloe ended up wrestling over a piece of toast and I was still brushing crumbs out of my hair when I got to school. Which was when I realised that I'd left my geography homework on the kitchen table. Even though I got into trouble about that, I still had a fun day with Lauren.

We managed to arrive at our maths lesson at the exact same time as Cute Josh. He actually smiled at us and said, 'Hi, Lauren. Hi, Lauren's friend.'

I was completely dazzled by how white his teeth were, but Lauren was very cool and said, 'This is

Amelia.' And he nodded as if that was a genuinely interesting piece of information for him. I tried nodding back, but I seemed to have lost control of my own neck and it ended up being quite a big nod, more of a bow really. Luckily, Josh had already turned away and sat down.

We took the seats across the aisle from him and, while we were working on the equations Mr Ireland put on the board, I noticed that Josh finished them nearly as quickly as Lauren, which is impressive because Lauren is very good at maths.

The first thing Milly said when we walked into the drama studio was, 'Oh good, you're here.' Which I thought was pretty rude. It's not like Lauren could help being sick before. When we got down to working on our scene, Milly agreed that Lauren could try being the mother for this lesson. She was excellent.

When the bell went, Jasveen said, 'That went really well.'

And we all looked at Milly.

Milly might be a bit bossy, but one of the things I love about her is that she's never selfish.

'You were brilliant,' Milly said to Lauren. She took a deep breath. 'You should definitely be the mother.'

'Thank you!' Lauren squealed and she pulled us all into a hug.

I really think our group's performance could be the best.

Later on, we had my favourite lesson, music, and Mr Garcia told us that at tomorrow's rehearsal he'd be choosing soloists.

'I know we've got a few concert singers in here so if you'd like to audition tomorrow then please can I ask you to put your name on this list.' He waved a clipboard about. 'I'll pass it round.' And he handed it to Mark on the front row who immediately passed it on as if it was something dirty he didn't want to touch. Some people are so immature.

Mr Garcia was in full rambling mode by the time the clipboard got to us. I had a quick look at who else was on the list. There were some good singers on there. I really hoped I was in with a chance; I love performing and it's so cool when you get to do it with a whole orchestra. I wrote my name in big letters and slid the list across the table to Lauren.

'I don't think I'm going to audition this time,' she whispered.

I stared at her. 'What do you mean?'

'I mean, I don't think I want a solo.'

Unbelievable. 'Why not? We love having solos.'

'Yeah, but you have to go to extra rehearsals and everything. Besides, you know me: I'm the shy and quiet type.'

That was obviously supposed to be a joke, but I didn't think it was very funny. What on earth was going on with her?

'And I know that spending time with Mr Garcia is always a treat, but I'm not sure I can deal with too many of his jazzy jumpers.' She crossed her eyes.

I couldn't take this in. Lauren and I had auditioned for every singing role possible ever since we started at St Mark's. Part of the reason we became best friends was because we were the two singing narrators in our Year Seven end-of-year show. 'So you're really not even going to audition?' I asked.

She shook her head. 'I just don't fancy it.'

Mr Garcia sent a laser look in our direction so I had to stop asking questions, even though I was absolutely certain that Lauren hadn't told me the real reason she didn't want to audition. Something weird was going on and I was determined to find out what.

But when the last bell went, and I finally got to speak to Lauren without being interrupted by an annoying teacher, she just brushed me off.

'Why don't you want a solo in the concert?' I asked while we were packing up our bags.

'I just don't,' she said.

'But we always audition for solos.'

'I'm just getting over the flu. I don't think I'm up to auditioning tomorrow.'

I looked at her. She was still very pale. If anything, she looked worse than she had that morning.

I squeezed her elbow. 'You should've just said if you were feeling ill again.'

'I'm not feeling ill!'

I dropped her arm.

'Sorry,' she said. 'I'm just tired. You don't need to worry. I'll still be in the concert; we'll have a good time, yeah?'

I was so surprised that she'd snapped at me that I hardly heard her.

She stuffed her arms into her coat. 'I've got to meet my mum in the car park. See you tomorrow.'

And she was gone.

I blinked a bit. Maybe I was being unfair; maybe Lauren was a bit washed out after being ill and I should just get over my disappointment that she wasn't up to auditioning for a solo. But I couldn't help remembering yesterday morning when Lauren had been insisting that she was perfectly fit.

I headed downstairs and out of the main entrance. There was a bit of a bottleneck where the path narrows and hundreds of kids were all rushing to get as far away from school as fast as they could and someone bumped me with their backpack. I swung round to tell them what I thought of them and found myself face to face with Cute Josh.

'Sorry, Amelia,' he said.

I opened my mouth to reply, but he was already moving away with his crowd of friends. Cute Josh had remembered my name. And we'd practically had an actual conversation. Lauren was going to be sorry she'd missed this. I pulled out my phone and sent her a quick text with a lot of exclamation marks.

Ella and I got to the gates, where Chloe was leaning against a tree, at the same time.

'Why are you two so crazy-happy?' Chloe asked us. 'You've both got a smile like when you put a quarter of an orange in your mouth.'

I looked at Ella. I hadn't noticed, but she did seem cheerful. Her eyes were bright and her cheeks were flushed.

'I wouldn't say I'm crazy-happy,' I said. To be honest, I was still confused by Lauren. But Josh had certainly cheered me up a bit. 'However, it's true that there are occasional moments in this soul-destroying dungeon of doom that don't suck all the joy out of me.'

'To be fair,' Chloe said, 'you weren't exactly full of joy to begin with.'

'True.' I turned to Ella. 'What about you?' I asked. 'What level of joy-suckage are you at?'

'I am pretty happy,' she admitted. 'Crystal has asked me to be her partner in hockey!'

She made it sound like a princess had invited her to a royal ball.

'Who's Crystal and what's so great about her?' I asked.

'Is she any good at hockey?' Chloe interrupted. 'Because if you've got a good partner then she can really help you work on your skills.'

'She is good at hockey and she's good in other ways too.'

'What ways?' I asked.

Ella screwed up her nose. 'Well ... she's really popular.'

'You're popular too, Ella,' Chloe pointed out. 'Your class chose you to be tutor captain, didn't they?'

When people pay Ella compliments, it's almost as if she doesn't hear them. She just carried straight on and said, 'I was surprised because I didn't even think that Crystal knew my name. Ashandra and

50

Kayleigh had already made a pair, so I thought I was going to be left on my own, but then Crystal asked me. She's ...' Ella struggled to find the words to tell us how wonderful this girl was. 'She's not at all scared of the teachers. And she always thinks of funny things to say when Kieran shouts out rude things and she does dancing competitions and she wears her hair in a fishtail plait and she's got pierced ears.'

I pulled a face. 'She sounds like one of those girls that does beauty pageants.'

'She's not like that. She's fun. And she'll definitely be able to help me with my hockey. I was really lucky that she chose me.'

I could feel the buzz of Josh speaking to me slipping away. I didn't like the idea of anyone lording it over Ella. Except me occasionally of course.

'I don't know why you're talking like she's a superstar and you're amazed that she's noticed you. You're good at lots of things too.'

Ella sighed. She obviously felt that we were missing the point. 'I'm just saying that she's very cool.'

'You're cool,' Chloe said.

And, even though I wouldn't have said that myself, I was glad that Chloe had.

'I'm not cool! I'm just normal. Crystal is like someone from the telly. Or America.'

I opened my mouth to say what I thought about Crystal, but Chloe interrupted me. She told us what happened when she went to see the head of PE to tell her she wasn't happy about not being allowed to try out for the rugby youth squad. It was a long story and, by the time Chloe had got to the point, we'd reached Dad's door and I rang the bell.

'So basically you're saying that Mrs Henderson told you there's nothing she can do,' Ella summed up.

'Yep,' Chloe said as Suvi was opening the door. 'She doesn't care at all.'

'Hello, girls.' Suvi smiled at us. 'Don't forget to take your shoes off. Who doesn't care?'

'The head of PE. She doesn't care that I can't be on the rugby youth squad.'

Suvi's smile disappeared. 'They still won't let you play? And this teacher will not help?'

'She says it's nothing to do with her.'

Suvi growled in her throat. Ella twitched. We'd never heard Suvi make that sort of noise.

'What a woman! How can she say this?'

Even Chloe was surprised by Suvi's reaction. 'Well, she doesn't actually run the squad or anything. It's run by th—'

'She's your teacher, yes? And you are a big strong girl. Very big, very strong and you wish to play rugby. How is it that she can say it's not her business? Doesn't she care that all the time girls are giving up sports because society is telling them to think about their nails instead? Does she know about all the talented women who cannot get funding to participate in their sports while they're throwing money at the mens?'

Normally, I correct Suvi when she makes a mistake in English, but somehow the words didn't come out. I concentrated on unzipping my coat.

'This makes me angry,' she muttered.

Nobody said anything. We could see she was angry. There were two pink spots on her freckled cheeks and it was one of the few times I'd ever heard her raise her voice. Suvi is a very calm person. She doesn't get angry when Kirsti screams. She doesn't get angry when Dad completely forgets what she's asked him to do. She didn't even get angry when I found out she and Dad were having a baby and I called her a cow.

Lucy popped out of the sitting room. 'What are you talking about?' she demanded. 'Why is Suvi all excited?'

'For some things you must shout. This isn't right

and it's making me angry that it's happening to someone special.'

Chloe looked surprised. 'Do you mean me?'

'Of course you. All you girls are special.'

Now I was surprised. I would never have expected Suvi to describe me as special.

'And this is important. You should never let someone tell you that you can't do something because you're a girl.'

'Yeah, but I've already said that,' Chloe said. 'It hasn't made any difference.'

'Sometimes just saying isn't enough. Sometimes you have to do as well.'

'Do what exactly?'

'Come with me,' said Suvi, drawing Chloe into the kitchen. 'I have some ideas.'

I pulled off my tie and settled down on the sofa. Lucy stretched out on the rug in front of me, her face screwed up in thought.

'What?' I asked her.

'There must be some things,' she said.

I put a cushion behind my back. 'What things?'

'Things that boys can do that girls can't.'

I rested my feet on the coffee table. 'I don't think so.'

'What about grow a beard?'

'Remember Mrs Russell?' Mrs Russell used to

babysit for us; she had more facial hair than Mr Russell.

'Oh, yeah. She had a beard didn't she?'

'And a moustache.' I took out my phone to see if Lauren had replied to my text about Josh, but she hadn't. Lucy got out her pens to draw Mrs Russell, only she got carried away with the hair and our old babysitter ended up more like that furry one from *Star Wars*. Chloe stayed in the kitchen with Suvi for a long time. I couldn't hear what they were saying, but they both looked a lot more cheerful when they came out.

After tea, I called Lauren to ask her when our biology homework was supposed to be in, but her mum said she was already in bed. Weird. It was only eight o'clock. I crossed my fingers that she wasn't getting ill again.

I ended up going to bed pretty early myself. Lucy barged into the bathroom while I was cleaning my teeth.

'Gor' 'posed to be 'sleep,' I said through the toothpaste foam.

'I nearly am,' she said, balancing on the edge of the bath in a very unsleepy way. 'But I thought of something boys can do that girls can't.'

I spat and rinsed. 'What?'

'Pee standing up.'

I pushed her out of the bathroom door. 'You can get a special adaptor to do that.'

'Really?' Her eyes bulged. 'I think I know what I want for Christmas.'

CHAPTER ✦ EIGHT

I probably wouldn't admit it, because everybody knows how much I hate school, but I actually like staying late for rehearsals. Once most pupils have gone home, the whole atmosphere of the building changes and I feel sort of special because I'm here working on something important.

I'd given Lauren the booklet of music and lyrics, and talked her through most of Mr Garcia's ramblings from last week, so, as long as Milly kept her big mouth shut, there was no reason for anyone to know that she'd missed the first rehearsal. Except Lauren didn't exactly do a good job of looking like an enthusiastic participant. She was slumped down in her chair, looking thoroughly bored. When Mr Garcia started the warm-up, I had to poke her to get her on her feet.

'Right,' said Mr Garcia, picking up a sheaf of papers. 'Time is moving on and we need to start working on solos, so this afternoon I would like to try out a few different voices.'

Mr Garcia always talks about 'voices' rather than the people they belong to. Sometimes he makes me feel like my voice is something separate from me. And more important.

'I'll leave you in Mr O'Brien's capable hands while I audition in the big practice room those of you looking for the responsibility of a larger role.' He looked down at his list. 'First on my list is ... Bartek Tarasewicz.'

Bartek stood up. He shook his long dark fringe out of his eyes and grinned. He didn't seem nervous at all. He only joined our school this year, but even on his very first day I remember him looking totally at home. He definitely had the confidence to be a good performer. I'd never heard him sing, but Milly told me that Olivia told her that he's got a great singing voice.

The rest of us started work on 'Walking in a Winter Wonderland' with Mr O'Brien. Even though I was standing right next to Lauren, I couldn't hear her singing. I stole a sideways glance at her. She was barely even moving her lips.

'What's the matter?' I whispered, but she just

jerked her head in Mr O'Brien's direction; he was staring right at us over the top of the piano. I didn't get it. Normally, she was so keen on singing. I looked at Lauren again; her face was tense and I wondered if she was in pain.

'Do you feel all right?' I asked.

'It's just a bit of a headache,' she muttered.

I was sorry she was hurting, but at least it explained her lack of enthusiasm. I'd been starting to think that she didn't want to do the concert at all.

Before I could ask her if she wanted to go home, Mr Garcia came back into the hall followed by Bartek. When Mr Garcia walks, his whole body is pulled up tight like a violin string whereas Bartek strolls along, smiling into the distance, like he's beside the sea on a sunny day. They looked so funny together that I nearly laughed. Then Mr Garcia called me to audition and my laugh turned to ice in my throat.

I wove my way between the other singers and followed Mr Garcia out of the hall and down the corridor to the practice room.

'I hope you don't mind an audience,' he said. 'I've got my sixth-form music group in, just so that they can give me the benefit of their opinions.' He opened the door and I was faced with five Year Thirteens sitting at a long table like an interview panel.

I wondered what Mr Garcia would say if I told him I did mind, but he clearly wasn't expecting any sort of reply. Almost all of the time that Mr Garcia talks, he just wants you to take in what he's saying without coming back with any thoughts of your own.

I don't normally mind singing in front of people; in fact, I love it. But, because I'd been thinking about this concert for so long and because I really, really wanted a solo, my heart started pumping hard and I could feel my face getting hot. I bit my lip; I had to control my nerves or I'd make mistakes and then there would be no chance of a good part.

Mr Garcia sat down at the piano. 'Let's hear what you've just been doing with Mr O'Brien,' he said, launching into the intro before I'd had a chance to nod in reply.

I pulled my spine up straight: it's important to be able to get as much air into your lungs as possible when you're singing. I listened to Mr Garcia carefully to make sure I came in at exactly the right moment. Halfway through the first line, I saw one of the Year Thirteens writing something down and I panicked; my voice wobbled and Mr Garcia looked up sharply, but I pulled it back and after that my body sort of went into automatic mode. When I was finished, Mr Garcia had me try a verse from two of the other songs. I didn't make any more really obvious mistakes but once he stopped to tell me how he would like the line and made me sing it again. I hoped I'd done that OK because it's really important that he knows that I can take direction.

When I finished the last song, the Year Thirteens clapped politely, but it was hard to tell what Mr Garcia thought. He just said, 'Thank you, Amelia,' and walked with me back to the hall to call out another name.

'How did it go?' Lauren asked as I slipped back into my place beside her.

'OK-ish.'

She gave me a big smile and held up crossed fingers, which made me think that at least she seemed to care about me being in the concert.

We had to sit through another hour of rehearsing the group numbers before Mr Garcia had finished all the auditions. He stood in front of us, holding his clipboard, and everyone was so keen to hear who had the solos that he didn't even have to ask for silence.

'Before I read out the names of the chosen few, I would like to remind you that in taking on a featured part you are also taking on a responsibility,' he began. 'I expect commitment and one hundred per cent attendance at the extra rehearsals. If you can't manage that then you will lose your part.' He cleared his throat. 'The solo in "Jingle Bell Rock" will be sung by Nathan Weisgard . . .'

Nathan did an air-guitar solo and tossed his long hair about like an eighties rock star, but I could hardly process the names being read out. Every part of me was focused in on hearing my own name. My heart had started to gallop again. I was jiggling my foot like I do when I've got a stomach ache. The further Mr Garcia got down the list, the more convinced I was that I wasn't going to have a special part. Lauren reached out and took my hand.

'"Baby, It's Cold Outside" – Bartek Tarasewicz and Amelia Strawberry.'

I couldn't help a small gasp. Lauren squeezed my hand hard as I smiled at her. I looked across at Bartek and he grinned back at me. I was so pleased. It was definitely my favourite song in the whole concert and, unlike some of the other solos where people only got a verse to themselves before the chorus came crashing in, Bartek and I were going to sing the whole thing by ourselves.

Mr Garcia reached the end of his list and dismissed us with more dire warnings about not missing rehearsals.

As we started to gather our stuff together, I turned to Lauren. 'How's your head?' I asked.

'It's better,' she said.

I didn't mean to go on about her not auditioning, but I couldn't help saying, 'I'm really sad you're not doing a solo too.'

She picked up her bag and stood up slowly. 'I really don't mind,' she said. But there was something brittle about her voice that made me think that perhaps she did. I tried to get a really good look at her face, but she was half turned away from me, staring down at the floor. 'In fact,' she said really quietly, 'I'm not sure that I'm going to bother with the concert this year.'

I sucked in my breath. 'What do you mean?'

'I don't think I want to be in it.' She finally looked up at me and it was as if she was begging me to understand. But I didn't understand at all.

'I thought you liked doing concerts,' I said.

She twisted her bag strap in her hands. 'I do. But you heard what Mr Garcia said about having to attend all the rehearsals. I think I've got an orthodontist appointment coming up and my mum said she might let me have a day off school to go Christmas shopping in London.'

I blinked. Lauren's mum didn't seem the type to let you miss school to go shopping. She always seems quite uptight about schoolwork.

'Couldn't you do that stuff on days when there aren't rehearsals?'

Lauren looked away again. 'I just think I'm going to give it a miss this year.'

It still didn't make any sense to me. 'We've been looking forward to doing this for ages.'

'You can still do it.'

'I wanted to do it with you!' I hadn't meant to say that quite so sharply but I couldn't believe that this was happening. 'Look,' I said trying to sound gentle, 'you've got a headache; it'll be more fun next week when you're better. Why don't you wait and see how you feel about it then?'

To my horror, Lauren clenched her jaw and stared fiercely out of the window. I was afraid she was going to cry.

'I'm not going to do this concert,' she said eventually. 'Please stop going on about it.'

And she looked so upset that I said, 'OK. If that's what you really want.' Even though I was totally confused about what was going on.

She took a long, shuddery breath and tried to smile. 'I'll still come and watch you,' she said. 'You're going to be brilliant. I can't wait to see you onstage.'

That was the first thing that she'd said all afternoon that sounded like she really meant it.

CHAPTER NINE

I thought about Lauren all that evening. I decided that there were only two possible explanations for her dropping out of the concert. Either she'd decided that she didn't like singing any more or she was feeling so ill that she didn't really know what she was saying. Since she'd looked so upset about the whole thing, I thought it was more likely that her headache had been messing with her. The most sensible and mature thing I could do would be not to push her on it until she was feeling better and then, just before next week's rehearsal, I could check that she was really sure about her decision. So the next morning I was super careful to keep the conversation completely away from singing.

*

We had a great day. Cute Josh sat in front of us in chemistry and we sketched the back of his head. (He's got a very nice neck.) Then we had French and Madame told us that it's possible to say a great deal with your eyes so Lauren and I spent the rest of the lesson trying to communicate by blinking and staring and rolling our eyes.

'Guess what this means,' I whispered, and I used my eyes to mime my powerful attraction to Cute Josh.

'Do you need something to be sick in?' Lauren asked.

We cracked up.

Our last lesson was biology and Lauren made a countdown of the minutes until we were free for the weekend. We took it in turns to strike the minutes off.

Lauren doodled an ice-cream sundae. *Let's go to the milkshake bar tomorrow* she wrote underneath.

I nodded. Then I added to Lauren's doodle so that it looked like she was paying for me to eat a truckload of sundaes.

When I woke up on Saturday morning, it was a relief to know that for the first time in weeks I was going out with Lauren and I didn't have to spend the day with my annoying sisters.

Usually, when we go into town, I call for Lauren and we catch the bus together, but she sent me a text to say that her mum was giving her a lift. I thought it was a bit mean of her mum not to offer to take me too – I only live five minutes away from them – but I'm used to Lauren's mum; she's not the super-friendly type. In fact, sometimes I think she doesn't like me very much.

So I got the bus by myself. The milkshake bar was pretty busy, but I managed to grab a table by the window. As I sat down, Lauren's mum's car pulled up outside. Lauren opened the door, but her mum carried on talking to her for ages. She didn't look too happy. Finally, Lauren climbed out of the car and came inside.

'Hi,' I said.

'Hi.' Her shoulders were tensed and she had dark circles under her eyes. I wondered if she'd been rowing with her mum.

'I really need chocolate,' she said, heading for the counter.

When we were sitting down with our shakes, I studied her face again.

'Are you all right?' I asked. 'You've got a scowl as if our darling headteacher has put you on litter duty.'

'Old Iron Hair Hamilton is nowhere near as bossy as my mother. She's driving me insane.'

'What's she doing?'

'She just keeps ... fussing. Matt's gone off to university and now my dad's away for work till next week, so it's just the two of us in the house and she's always worrying about me. It's revolting.'

'Have you told her to stop?'

Lauren stirred her shake with her straw. 'Hmm, trying to tell my mum not to do something is like trying to tell the tide not to come in. She doesn't want me to do anything or go anywhere.'

'At least you're here now.'

Lauren made a snorty noise and I got the impression that her mum hadn't even wanted her to meet me, which seemed odd because even though Lauren's mum has always been a bit of a fusser she's never had a problem with the milkshake bar before. What did she think was going to happen? That the cows would launch a protest about us glugging their milk and storm the building? I wondered if Lauren's mum was just lonely. Lauren's dad goes away for his work a lot and now Matt had gone to university, so perhaps she wanted Lauren around to talk to. But it didn't seem fair to stop Lauren doing anything for that reason.

We sipped our shakes and talked about parents and how ridiculous they are. I was telling Lauren about the time my dad made me put on his huge, ugly coat after we'd been swimming and anyone could've seen me, when someone tapped on the window. I looked up and saw Jasveen and Milly waving like toddlers who've had too much sugar. I gestured for them to come in.

'Hey!' Jasveen beamed, striding towards us.

'Hi.' I smiled.

Lauren muttered a hello, but she didn't look too happy. I wondered if Milly had done something new to annoy her.

'So what are you two up to?' Milly asked.

'We're fighting off a zombie invasion,' I said in my best deadpan voice.

Lauren nodded. 'Yeah, only both our weapons and the zombies are so small that they're invisible to the naked eye.'

Jasveen snorted. 'Is that mint chocolate?' she asked Lauren. 'Can I have a slurp?'

Lauren held out her shake.

'I meant, what are you doing after you've finished here?' Milly asked. 'Because we're going bowling and Faye Wright said that she heard that Bradley's going bowling for his birthday this afternoon. So . . .'

'He'll be there with his friends,' Jasveen finished. She rolled her eyes. 'Personally, I'm going for the bowling, not for the boys. You two should come and then I'll have someone to talk to while Milly's gawping.'

My interest was definitely piqued. Not by the bowling but because Bradley was friends with Josh. Not best friends but definitely friendly enough to have invited him to his party. I looked at Lauren; I was hoping to communicate all this to her through a look, but she was just staring into her milkshake.

'Shall we go, Loz?' I asked.

Lauren looked up. 'I don't know,' she said.

'Go on,' Milly said. 'It'll be brilliant.' She grabbed Lauren by the shoulders and shook her a little bit, 'Come on, sleepyhead, say yes. It'll wake you up a bit.'

'Don't!' Lauren snapped, jerking away from her.

'All right, keep your hair on! I was just saying you could do with some fun; you've been walking around looking miserable all week.'

'She's been ill,' I said.

'I thought she was supposed to be better.'

'I'm right here!' Lauren interrupted. 'Just because I don't want to go bowling to stare at some boys like a dribbling idiot doesn't mean there's anything wrong with me.'

I had no idea how this had suddenly turned into an argument.

'Are you calling me an idiot?' Milly asked.

'No,' Lauren said. 'I didn't mean that. I just don't feel—'

'Because you're the idiot. I know you think you're too cool and sarcastic to ever get excited about stuff, but that doesn't mean you have to take the mickey out of me.'

'I don't think she meant it like that,' I said.

'Don't tell me what I mean!' Lauren said, and she snatched up her coat and walked out of the bar.

Milly gave Jasveen a significant look.

I tried desperately to think of some way to explain Lauren's behaviour.

'She's having a really hard time with her mum at the moment,' I said. 'And you did lay it on a bit thick, Milly.'

Milly pursed her lips. 'Whatever. We all know she's being weird at the moment.'

'She's fine,' I said. Even though really I agreed with Milly. 'I've got to go after her.'

Jasveen gave me a half-smile. 'See you at school,' she said.

'Yeah, see you.'

Milly didn't say anything.

Lauren was sitting at the bus stop halfway down the road. She must have run there because she was out of breath when I got to her.

'You OK?' I asked.

'Yes. I'm just sick of Milly being so bossy.'

I didn't want to side with Milly but I didn't entirely understand what had happened. 'She just thought we might like to go bowling,' I said.

'Yeah and then she started shaking me and calling me dopey.'

'I don't think she meant to be horrible.' I hesitated. 'And you did sort of call her an idiot.'

'A dribbling idiot,' Lauren said, starting to laugh. When she'd got her breath back, she shook her head. 'I shouldn't have said that.'

'You know what Milly's like: she'll have forgotten about it in a minute. We could still catch up with them. If you want?'

Lauren's shoulders sagged. 'I don't really feel like going bowling.'

'We don't have to actually bowl; we could just go and hang out. I reckon Josh will be there, don't you?'

'I suppose so.'

'Go on, it'll be fun.'

I thought for a moment that she was going to say yes, but then Lauren shook her head. 'I've got some stuff to do at home. You go if you like.'

But I couldn't really. She seemed upset about something and it didn't feel right to leave her. 'Do you want to go and look in the shops instead?' I asked.

She shook her head again. 'I think I need

something to eat. How about lunch at my house?'

So we ended up going back on the bus, even though it was still early. When I tried to get to the bottom of why she'd kicked off at Milly, she just shrugged and mumbled. We got off the bus and walked to Lauren's house; when her mum opened the door, she took one look at Lauren and said, 'Why didn't you call me to pick you up?'

I turned to Lauren. I supposed those circles under her eyes did make her look a bit rough. But she hadn't said she didn't feel well.

Lauren's mum didn't wait for an answer. She pulled Lauren into the house. 'I told you this wasn't a good idea.'

'Mum!' Lauren snapped. 'Amelia, do you mind if you don't come in? I'm a bit tired.'

I barely had a chance to nod before her mum shut the door in my face. Rude.

I thought about going back to the bowling alley, but I didn't want Lauren to think I was siding with Milly; besides, I couldn't really afford another bus fare. So I ended up trailing home again.

When I got in, Mum was marking some homework for her class so I thought I'd keep up my attempts at being less selfish and tackle the mountain of washing in the laundry basket, since I had nothing else to do.

I was hanging socks on the radiator to dry, and wondering if Lauren's mum was just making a fuss or if Lauren was going to be ill again, when Ella got home from spending the day at her new friend Crystal's house. Chloe was supposed to be helping me, but she was more interested in seeing if she could make Lucy's tights big enough to fit her by tying them to the doorknob and stretching them across the room.

'How was the fabulous Crystal's house?' I asked Ella. 'Does she have one of those glass cabinets for all the trophies she's won for shiniest teeth and largest tiara collection?'

'No,' Ella said and picked up a handful of socks from the basket and took them to the other radiator to hang up.

'Did you have fun though?' Chloe asked.

'Mmm,' Ella said.

Ella doesn't get her acting skills from me. It was obvious she hadn't enjoyed herself. When I have a miserable time, I always tell people about it; in fact, I like telling people; sometimes I even make it sound worse than it actually was just so I can give them a really good story. I'd already told Mum and Chloe all about Lauren making us miss out on bowling. But Ella isn't like me; she tries to be happy all the time and she tries to always say yes to the questions she's asked.

Chloe gave Lucy's tights another yank. 'What did you do?'

'We went on her trampoline and then we watched a film. She's got this room that's like a mini cinema; there are four sofas in there and a screen that takes up half the wall.'

I was pretty determined not to be impressed by Crystal so I didn't say anything but I definitely wouldn't mind having a mini cinema in our house.

'Wow,' Chloe said. 'That sounds awesome.'

'Yeah,' Ella said. 'It was pretty cool.'

But it still seemed like there was something that wasn't cool.

Chloe was studying her face. 'Was the film too scary for you?'

Ella shook her head.

'Did you have to eat something you didn't like?'

'No, we had pizza.'

Chloe held Ella's arm. 'Was Crystal mean to you? Because if she was I'm going to have a lot to say to her.'

'She really wasn't; she gave me her new pencil.'

Chloe looked at me, but I couldn't think of any reasons why someone who had just watched a film in a mini cinema while eating pizza with their friend would be unhappy either. So I said, 'What's the matter?'

'Nothing. I'm fine.'

'You don't look fine. You look like you're trying not to cry because something has upset you. Did it?'

She shrugged.

'Did Crystal do something?'

'Well . . .' Ella knitted her fingers together. 'She was a bit rude to her mum.'

Crazy. All this fuss was about manners. 'Don't worry about that. Chloe's rude to our mum all the time,' I pointed out.

'I'm not!' Chloe insisted. 'You're the rude one. You're the one that's always telling people they look awful and that wearing yellow makes them look like a blob of mustard.'

'I've been thinking about that and actually your jumper doesn't make you look like mustard.'

'Good.'

'It makes you look like one of Kirsti's poos.'

'See? You *are* rude!' And she pulled so hard on Lucy's tights that they pinged off the doorknob and she crashed into a chair.

I snorted.

'And rude again,' Chloe said, rubbing her hip.

'Well, obviously I'm rude to you. You're my sister and you behave like an ape so I'd have to be made of stone not to make jokes about that, but you're the one that's rude to Mum: you eat her best biscuits and you moon her.'

Ella helped Chloe pick the chair up. 'I don't mean the bare-bum kind of rude; it was more like Crystal telling her mum to shut up.'

Chloe's jaw dropped. 'Did she actually say that?'

Ella nodded.

'What did her mum say?' I asked.

Ella sat down on the sofa. 'Nothing really. That was part of what was horrible; it was as if her mum was just used to it because Crystal talks to her like that all the time.'

Chloe was attempting to wriggle into Lucy's tights. 'Maybe it's a joke; maybe that's how they talk in her family.'

'It just . . . made me feel uncomfortable.'

It seemed a little bit silly for Ella to be getting upset about someone else's bad behaviour. I gave her arm a squeeze. 'It's not worth worrying about it. If Crystal's mum wasn't upset then you shouldn't be either.'

But Ella was still frowning.

Then Chloe tried to do the splits and her bottom finally fought its way out of Lucy's tights with a loud *rrrrrrrrrip* and even Ella had to laugh.

CHAPTER ❤ TEN

'Is Lauren not in today?' Milly asked on Monday morning.

'I haven't seen her yet,' I said. Lauren hadn't texted me to say she was ill and I was still hoping she might turn up. But after we'd finished registration and got half an hour into the first lesson I had to admit to myself that it didn't seem likely she'd be coming in today.

I couldn't concentrate on the book in front of me. I was fed up. Angry. If Lauren was off sick again, why hadn't she told me?

School seemed to drag on even longer than it usually does, but as soon as I got outside after the final bell I fished my mobile out of the bottom of my bag and called Lauren.

It took a while for her to answer. 'Hi,' she said as if everything was fine.

'Why didn't you tell me you weren't coming to school?' I asked.

'Sorry, I just felt really rough this morning. I would've texted you, but I've been asleep most of the day.'

'What's the matter with you? Have you been sick?'

'No, I'm just really tired.'

'Have you been to the doctor?'

She sighed. 'I'm not that bad, honestly.'

There was a pause. 'So you'll be in tomorrow?' I asked.

'I . . . I don't think so.'

'Lauren! I thought you said you didn't feel that bad. We've got drama tomorrow. I'll never hear the end of it from Milly if you're not there.'

'Milly can go stuff herself.'

I didn't think it was fair to be turning on Milly again. 'Well, actually, I can sort of see where she's coming from. You promised you'd be there. It's not surprising that Mil—'

'Can you stop going on about Milly?'

'All right, all right, but I don't really understand what your problem with her is.'

'I don't care about Milly!'

I didn't know why she was getting so worked up. 'If you're not mad with Milly, why didn't we go bowling on Saturday?'

'I told you; I didn't feel like it.'

Her voice was hard. I couldn't believe she was getting snippy with me.

'But maybe I did,' I said. 'And maybe it would've been nice if you'd asked me what I thought.'

'Oh, I am sorry! I do apologise for being ill.'

'What do you mean? You never said you were ill on Saturday.'

'Maybe I couldn't get a word in edgeways because you were going on and on about drama scenes and stupid pigging singing!'

That was so unfair and she knew it. I'd asked her several times on the bus if she was all right and every time she'd brushed me off.

'You used to like "stupid pigging" singing. I'm sorry if I'm getting too childish for you. Forget about coming to the concert if it's too much bother.'

She sucked in her breath. 'Amelia! Don't be like that. Of course I'm coming to the concert. I do care about it. I even care about this daft drama scene.'

'So you'll come in tomorrow?'

'I *can't*. Honestly, Amelia, I'm really sick; there's no way I'll be able to.'

I was totally confused. 'You said you weren't that bad!'

Lauren made a choking noise. 'I . . . It's . . . Oh, you don't understand!'

'No, I don't understand because you keep saying different stuff. Are you ill or not?'

'I'm too ill to come into school tomorrow,' she said in a tight voice. 'I'm sorry I'll miss drama.'

But she didn't sound sorry. She sounded angry. Well, I was angry too; I felt like she wasn't telling me everything. 'Lauren, what's going on?' I asked. 'Is this because of your fight with Milly?'

'No!'

'Is there some reason you don't want to come into school? Because everybody feels like they'd rather be lazing around at home sometimes, but—'

'Is that what you think? That I'm just lazy?'

I hadn't meant that at all and now she was cross with me again. Something inside me snapped like a brittle twig.

'I don't know!' I shouted. 'I don't know what to think because you won't tell me anything!'

'Think whatever you want to, Amelia.'

And she hung up.

I blinked hard. My hands were shaking.

I'd been walking all the time I'd been talking and I was already quite far from school. I didn't backtrack to see if Ella and Chloe were still waiting for me at the school gates; instead, I stormed home

81

by myself. The other two didn't arrive for another fifteen minutes.

'You could've told us you weren't walking with us,' Chloe said when she found me in the kitchen. 'We waited ages for you.'

'So?' I snapped.

'So it's not very polite.'

'Your face isn't very polite.'

'Sorry, is this better?' And she pushed her nose into a piggy snout and stuck out her tongue.

'Do you have to be such an immature, blob-headed moron?'

Ella stepped between us. 'It's just that we weren't sure whether we should keep waiting,' she said. 'We were a bit worried.'

'You're always worried, Ella. I can't be held responsible for that.'

Chloe would have snapped back at me, but Ella just turned away. As she did, I saw her face pucker like she was about to cry.

I stomped upstairs and threw myself on my bed. I was so angry inside that I wanted to be able to lash out at someone. I was trying to find reasons to be mad at Chloe and Ella, but really I had to admit that they hadn't done anything wrong. I knew I was taking my bad mood out on them.

I breathed hard and clenched my fists. I was so

annoyed. Mostly with myself. I thought I'd decided not to be the mean big sister any more and here I was saying horrible things to sweet little Ella. The point about deciding to behave well is that it takes more than just good intentions. It's really easy to think that you're going to be a better person, but then you get into the heat of the moment and it's actually quite hard to control your feelings. I sighed. I couldn't go back to being the stroppy one now. Things were all weird with Lauren, but for once I was determined that I wasn't going to spread my bad feelings all over my family. I was going to be considerate.

I took a few deep breaths and went back downstairs.

'I'm sorry I shouted at you, Ella,' I said.

She looked startled. I suppose she hasn't heard me say sorry very much. 'That's all right.'

Chloe looked at me. 'And I'm sorry I called you names,' I said to her.

'Apology accepted, gorilla-breath,' she said.

It's funny how there are a lot of different ways to call people names and some of them are OK and some are not.

Chloe filled the kettle at the sink. 'Do you want a cup of tea, poop-for-brains?'

I let her get away with that one.

CHAPTER ◆ ELEVEN

Lauren wasn't in school the next day and she didn't call me either. Which was fine because I didn't want to speak to her anyway. Since I'd decided I wasn't going to be a misery guts who upset her family any more, I didn't tell Mum or Chloe or anyone about falling out with Lauren; instead, I focused on being helpful and not grumpy. So when Mum got back from school I volunteered to make tea while she had a bath. I was halfway through when I heard Lucy squealing in the sitting room.

'Quick! Quick! Come and look!' she shouted.

That's the sort of thing she says when she's taken off a plaster or found a hairball the size of a melon under the sofa, but I put down the knife I was using and stuck my head into the sitting room just in case it was actually something interesting for once. Lucy was pointing at the TV and Chloe was standing frozen in front of it. On the screen was a boy's wide, grinning face. Thunder.

It was a local news feature on the new youth squad and how they hoped they were training the stars of future Rugby World Cups. It only lasted thirty seconds, but Thunder did get to say that he thought the coaching at the club was 'awesome'.

'You didn't tell us Thunder was going to be on the telly,' I said to Chloe.

'I didn't know,' she said in a tight voice. 'I didn't know because he didn't tell me and he didn't tell me because he's the worst friend in the world.' She clenched her jaw and her fists.

'Or maybe he was afraid to tell you because he knew you'd look like that,' I said. I hoped she wasn't going to start punching things because somehow, whenever one of my sisters starts trashing the place, it's me that gets the blame because I'm the oldest. Like that means I can keep any of them in check.

'Or maybe he forgot about it,' Lucy said. 'Maybe he had other things in his head. He does spend lots of time talking about what's for tea. I forget about stuff when I'm thinking about important things. Like sweets or turning into a dinosaur.'

Chloe wasn't listening. 'I can't believe it.

Thunder gets to do everything. He gets to be on the squad and on TV. I'm better at rugby than him! I'd be better on TV as well.'

I actually felt sorry for Chloe; it did seem really unfair. 'You totally would,' I agreed. 'Your whole face could fit on the screen and, unlike Thunder, your nose looks nothing like a potato.'

She twitched out of her trance.

'Yours is more like a carrot,' I went on.

She gave a half-smile. 'Yeah, well, at least I haven't got cauliflower ears like you.'

'No, you just smell like Brussels sprouts.'

Then she twisted my arm behind my back and I knew I'd managed to cheer her up.

'What are you going to say to Thunder?' I asked, shaking her off.

She flexed her muscles. 'I'll just let my fists do the talking.'

I was pretty sure that she was mostly joking. 'Seriously though, don't fall out with him. You two have only just got things sorted out after you said you didn't want to go out with him.'

'I know and after he stopped all that nonsense we agreed that we were going to stay as best friends. Friends are supposed to tell each other things.'

'It *is* quite hard to tell people things when you know they're going to be cross,' Lucy said. 'Like when the arm popped off that old doll of Mum's. I didn't want to say because she'd shout at me.'

Chloe and I looked at each other.

'Lucy!' Chloe said. 'You broke Annabella and didn't tell anyone?'

Lucy stared calmly back at us. 'That's what I'm saying. I didn't tell so Mum wouldn't be cross with me.'

'When did this happen?' I asked.

'Last week.'

'You mean Mum's got no idea that her most precious thing from when she was little has lost an arm?' Chloe demanded.

Lucy nodded.

'You'd better show me,' I said to Lucy. 'And if I can't fix it then you're going to have to confess.'

Lucy scowled, but we made her tiptoe upstairs so Mum wouldn't hear us from the bathroom. She showed us where she'd hidden poor Annabella under her bed. I managed to squeeze her little plastic arm into its socket and then I snuck into Mum's bedroom and quickly put her back in her box in Mum's wardrobe, before Mum got out of the bath.

'No more touching Annabella till you're twenty-five,' I said to Lucy.

Lucy tutted. 'I'll be practically dead by then.'

'Good. Maybe you'll be too weak to break her again.'

'I think you'd better go and tidy the Pit to make up for what you've done,' Chloe said to Lucy.

My mum still calls our basement room the playroom but the rest of us call it the Pit because it's always such a mess in there with books and toys all over the floor and all the furniture that's too shabby to be anywhere else in the house. Actually, during half-term, Lucy had completely tidied and redecorated the whole room because she had this crazy idea that Dad, Suvi and Kirsti could live there. It was really sad to realise that Lucy wants to live with Kirsti so much that she was prepared to spend hours tidying up all that mess. Obviously, Mum and Dad had to explain that Kirsti wouldn't be coming to live with us and, in the weeks since that happened, the creeping tide of tiny plastic toys has already washed back over the floor of the Pit.

'Good idea,' I said to Chloe. 'Having to sort out Sylvanian shoes from Lego pieces and My Little Pony brushes is enough to drive anyone to good behaviour.'

We went back into the kitchen and Chloe helped me finish making the chilli.

'I could understand him not wanting to tell me

'bad news,' she said while crunching on a piece of red pepper.

'Are we back to Thunder?' I asked.

'Yes. Bad news I understand, but you'd think he'd want to share good news with me, like being on TV.'

I searched in the drawer for the tin-opener. 'But, if he had, what would you've said?'

'I'd have said, "That's really unfair. I'm better at rugby than you and I ought to be the one on TV."'

'Hmm.'

'But then I might've been able to say, "I saw you on TV and your voice only squeaked a little bit when you were talking to the interviewer."'

'He'll be sorry to have missed out on such high praise.'

Chloe shook her head. 'Friends are supposed to share things.'

She had a good point. I stirred a tin of tomatoes into the pot and wondered why Lauren didn't seem to want to share things with me any more.

'Maybe you should talk to him about it?' I suggested.

'Oh, I will. This is all he's going to hear about tomorrow.'

Maybe I should take my own advice and talk to Lauren. I missed her. But she was the one who was being unreasonable. She should be calling me. I pushed thoughts about my best friend out of my head and went back to the chilli.

Later, when we were in bed, Chloe whispered, 'Suvi says I shouldn't give up on getting girls on the rugby squad. Do you think she's crazy?'

I do think Suvi is a little crazy. I used to think that she was crazy-mean and that she'd stolen my dad away from my mum; now I know that's not true but I still think she's a bit crazy; she doesn't eat sugar and she likes maths and she says TV is bad for you, but I don't mind those things so much any more.

'You'd have to be crazy to want to be a part of this family,' I said.

'Yeah, but I mean about the rugby squad. She says that I should make them put girls on the squad; I can't do that, can I?'

I wriggled further down under my duvet. 'I don't know. Can you?'

'I don't know.'

'Maybe you should find out.'

CHAPTER ✦ TWELVE

The next morning, Milly actually managed not to make any comments about Lauren during drama. But somehow that was even worse. She was wearing a special face like she thought she was being all saintly and gracious because she was being kind enough not to point out the fact that Lauren had let us all down.

I wondered if Lauren really was still ill or if she was just avoiding me. I sort of wanted to call her, but I couldn't quite get my thoughts about the whole situation to make sense. Part of me wanted to say sorry, but a bigger part of me thought that she ought to apologise first.

I still hadn't sorted things out in my mind when Chloe, Ella and I got to Dad's house. Lucy was sprawled on the stairs, arranging My Little Ponies in a battle scene with various home-made weapons and sucking a lollipop.

'Where did you get that?' I asked.

'I made it out of a Smarties tube.'

'Not the pony bazooka. The lollipop.' Suvi never usually allows anything that sugary in the house.

'Emily gave it to me.'

'Evil Emily?'

'Yep. Evil Emily's got a grandma who buys her lots of sweets because she knows that it annoys her mum.'

'I suppose that's the best kind of Evil Emily.'

Lucy slurped happily. 'And I've got a packet of Maltesers from Rose.'

'Why are your friends being so generous all of a sudden?'

Lucy shrugged and squished a blob of Blu-Tack on to a tiny plastic hand grenade so she could stick it to a pony hoof. 'Cos I'm nice.'

I stepped over the battlefield to go upstairs. 'It can't possibly be that.'

Before we went to bed, Dad told me and Chloe to put all the recycling out on the kerb.

I wasn't in the best of moods. 'Why do we have to do it?' I asked.

'It's important for you to learn life skills,' Dad

said. 'Next week, I'm going to teach you how to change a tyre.'

'I can already do that,' Chloe said. 'Thunder's uncle showed us.'

'What about you, Amelia?' Dad asked. 'What are you going to do when you find yourself with a flat tyre by the side of the motorway?'

'I'll ring Chloe.' I folded my arms. 'Anyway, what has this got to do with recycling?'

Dad sat back and opened his paper. 'I told you: life skills.'

'I'm pretty sure I can carry some cardboard boxes without any practice, but I can see that even a short walk might crumble your elderly bones so just this once I'll do it.' I followed Chloe to the garage before he could say anything. I didn't really mind that much about moving some recycling; I just felt so fed up about Lauren.

The recycling is supposed to go in a little green bin in the garage, but that quickly gets full up. Some people, like Suvi and Ella, neatly stack the extra stuff round the bin, but other people, i.e. everybody else, just open the door from the kitchen and toss it into the garage. Which means, when it's collection time, you have to crawl about in the cold garage, fishing yoghurt pots out from whatever they've rolled under.

I tried to pick up an armful of plastic bottles, but they escaped my grasp and clattered all over the concrete floor. I huffed.

'Why don't you make up with Lauren?' Chloe asked.

'Who says I need to make up with Lauren?'

'Well, it's obvious you've fallen out with someone. And, since you haven't been spending hours and hours on the phone to her, I'm pretty sure it's Lauren.'

My skin prickled. Infuriating. I'd put so much effort into not taking my bad mood out on my family, but obviously I hadn't done a very good job. I bit my lip.

'If you make up with her then you could stop being super grumpy all the time and just go back to being your normal level of grumpy.'

I couldn't help giving Chloe a black look. 'If Lauren wants to make up, she knows where I am.'

'Yeah, but you said she's poorly. Why don't you go round? You could do it tomorrow after rehearsal.'

'I'm not going back there; it's bad enough that her mum makes me feel unwelcome, but if Lauren doesn't want to see me then I won't set foot in that place again!'

Chloe stomped on a juice carton to make it pop. 'Yeah you will.'

'I won't. I'm furious.'

'I know you are. But you get furious about things all the time; you were furious this morning when I used your toothbrush.'

I stared at her. 'Was that you? You said it was Lucy.'

Chloe went on gathering up packaging. 'I said Lucy had used it, which was true, but that doesn't mean that I didn't use it too. It's the only one that's ever in the proper place. I don't have time to remember what I've done with my toothbrush the night before when I'm trying to get ready for school.'

I made a growling noise in my throat.

'Anyway, the thing is that you were angry then, but you've completely forgiven me now, haven't you? Especially since I'm offering you such good advice about Lauren.'

'Who I am still furious with.'

'But what I'm saying is that you get cross with people about ten times a day. You like it. You'll have forgotten about it by tomorrow.'

'Maybe. But I'm pretty fed up of her not being a very good friend.'

'She is ill though, isn't she? She keeps being ill. She had all that time off before half-term.'

'That wasn't all being ill,' I said. 'She had to go

95

to a wedding and some days she had to go to the orthodontist.'

'I didn't know they let you have a whole day off for that. Anyway, she seems pretty sicky. She always looks dead pale when I see her. What exactly is wrong with her?'

'Nothing,' I said. But in my head I could hear Lauren saying, *I'm really sick*. 'She just gets tired sometimes,' I said. 'It's because of when she had glandular fever.'

'I thought she had that ages ago.'

I wished Chloe would stop going on. 'She should just go to the doctor and get them to give her something for it,' I said, shoving the garage door open a lot harder than necessary. Chloe carried out the jam-packed green bin while I followed with a cardboard box crammed with the rest of the recycling.

'Maybe there's nothing the doctors can do,' Chloe said. 'Remember Nana?'

It was awful when they told us that there wasn't anything they could give Nana to make her better. 'This is completely different. Lauren's not really that ill and she isn't going to die.'

'But still, sometimes even doctors can't make people completely right again, can they?'

I didn't say anything.

'And school are letting her not come in, aren't they?'

I remembered Lauren saying that school had sent home our drama play for her to read.

Chloe upended the little green bin into the big green bin. 'You'd have to be pretty pigging sick to get old Iron Hair to let you off school.'

'I suppose.'

Chloe flipped the lid of the big bin closed 'See? You're not furious now, are you?'

She was right. I wasn't cross any more. I was worried.

CHAPTER ✿ THIRTEEN

I fretted about Lauren all the next day. Finally, I decided that I'd go round to see her after rehearsal. While we were waiting for Mr Garcia and Mr O'Brien, I sat with Milly, Olivia and Bethany. Everyone was talking about Nathan's haircut. Last week, when Mr Garcia announced he'd got a solo, Nathan was flicking his shoulder-length hair about, but now he'd had it all cut off so short that he looked like he'd joined the army. We were still staring when Mr Garcia clapped his hands for quiet and got us started on warm-up exercises.

I wasn't concentrating on singing as hard as I should have been. I lost my place a couple of times when we were singing the group songs, but luckily Mr O'Brien didn't notice. It was probably a good thing that Mr Garcia had told me and Bartek that we wouldn't be working on our duet until next week.

Bartek was sitting behind us and, while Mr O'Brien was hunting for some music, he leant forward and said, 'We're going to sing great, yeah?'

I turned round. He was grinning at me and I couldn't help smiling back. Bartek always looks so cheerful. I bet he doesn't tie himself in knots worrying about stuff. 'If we don't sing well I'm pretty sure Mr Garcia will tell us,' I said.

'I hear he is very angry with bad singing.'

'Yep.' I nodded. 'He screams and pouts and dishes out horrible punishments.'

Bartek slowly moved his eyes sideways. I followed his gaze; he was looking at Nathan. 'Maybe Nathan isn't singing so good and Mr Garcia . . .' He mimed a pair of scissors.

I burst out laughing.

'We must be good,' he said. 'Because this is nice.' He tugged my hair. 'And this . . .' he ran a hand through his shiny black hair in a silly shampoo ad kind of way, 'is even nicer.'

Mr O'Brien crashed some chords to get us to be quiet at that point, but I thought that rehearsing with Bartek was going to be fun.

*

On the way to Lauren's house, I tried to plan what I wanted to say. I was going to start off with what I knew I'd done wrong: I shouldn't have made such a fuss about not going bowling and I should have been more understanding about her being ill. Except I was a bit confused about just how ill she was. I felt like I should have asked her about it more. But I had *tried*. Mostly she just kept saying she was fine. What if Chloe was right and there was something seriously wrong? I was getting in a tangle again. Once I'd said sorry, I really needed some straight answers from Lauren.

I rang the doorbell and waited. Through the glass panels I saw Lauren's mum coming towards me. For a minute, I wished I was Jasveen: she's one of those nice, polite girls that parents always love; she'd know the right way to start this conversation off.

Lauren's mum opened the door and I hesitated. It seemed quite formal to say 'Hello, Mrs Anderson,' but she'd never asked me to call her by her first name so I didn't feel like I could do that either.

'Hi,' I said eventually.

'Amelia,' she said. Not even 'Hello, Amelia'. Just my name in a cross, teacherish sort of voice.

I swallowed. 'How's Lauren?'

'Asleep. She's worn out.'

'Oh. I was hoping to talk to her.'

'That's not possible right now.'

I wanted to leave a message, but something about the way Lauren's mum was glaring at me made my words clog in my throat. I was going to have to sort this out by phone away from Lauren's mum's accusing eyes. I half turned to go.

'And Amelia?'

I looked back at her.

'All this . . .' she cast about for the right word, '. . . drama,' she said as if drama was the most revolting thing she could think of. 'This friendship drama isn't helping Lauren. She was extremely upset after you phoned her on Monday. You know she's really very ill and she needs rest. If you can't be a reliable friend then it might be best if you spent less time with her.'

What did she mean Lauren was really very ill? I was so shocked by what she'd said that I was completely robbed of speech. She'd got it all wrong. Lauren had said she was ill that one time and after that she kept playing it down as if it was nothing serious, but I was so upset and confused that I didn't have the words to explain this to Lauren's mum. All I could think of was that I had to get away as fast as I could. For some stupid reason, I said politely, 'Goodbye, Mrs Anderson,' as if her opinion of my manners meant anything now. She'd obviously got me down as the worst friend in the world. I walked blindly back up their drive and towards my house.

The more it rolled around in my head, the more bewildered I was. Lauren's mum thought I was a horrible person and that I was rowing with Lauren when she was sick. Why hadn't Lauren explained to me properly? What exactly did 'really very ill' mean? Ill like glandular fever or was it something worse?

When I got home, I went up to my bedroom and thought long and hard about what to do. I really needed to see Lauren, but her mum was clearly going to get in the way of that. I picked up my phone. What if Lauren was still asleep and her mum answered her mobile? What if no one answered and I had to leave a message? What would I say? Finally, I found a piece of paper and pen and tried to write something down. I crossed bits out and added things until I ended up with something that I thought was OK.

Dear Lauren,

I am so sorry that I shouted at you on Monday. I don't really care about not going bowling, but I am sad that we've fallen out because you're my best friend and I don't want to upset you.

I came round today but your mum said you were sleeping. She also said that you're really ill and she

seemed to think I knew all about it. Lauren, please
tell me what's wrong with you. I'm not cross that
you haven't told me, I just want to know because I
want to be there for you. I hope you know that you
can tell me absolutely anything and, whatever it is,
I'll always be your best friend.

Love Amelia xxx

P.S. Can I come and see you?

I decided it was best not to mention how mean her mum had been. I copied the whole thing out, put it in an envelope and slipped it into my bag so I could deliver it on the way to school.

In the morning, I snuck the letter through Lauren's door without her mum pouncing on me and then, in the middle of maths, I felt my phone vibrating in my pocket. When Mr Ireland turned his back, I slipped it out and took a quick look under the table. It was a text from Lauren.

I'm sorry too. I really want to talk to you. Can you come round tomorrow at ten?

I felt my shoulders relax. Maybe now this could finally be sorted out.

CHAPTER ✦ FOURTEEN

It was our weekend at Dad's so, in the morning, he gave me a lift to Lauren's house. After I'd got out of the car, it took me a moment to work up the courage to walk down the drive. I couldn't help thinking about the previous Saturday, when I'd woken up feeling so cheerful, compared to the sinking feeling I had in my stomach now. I was afraid of what kind of reception Lauren's mum was going to give me. What if she just told me to go away again? But I had to talk to Lauren so I marched up to their door and pressed the bell firmly.

After all that, it was Lauren's dad who opened the door.

'Hello, Amelia,' he said. 'Lauren's upstairs; go on up.'

'Thanks.' I don't see Lauren's dad that much because he's always travelling for his job but he's definitely a lot friendlier than her mum.

Upstairs, Lauren's bedroom door was closed. Normally, I'd have walked right in, but for some reason I knocked.

'Come in,' Lauren said.

I pushed open the door.

She was lying in bed, propped up on pillows. She looked awful.

'You look awful,' I said. My heart was off at a gallop again. What if there really was something horribly wrong with her?

'Thanks,' Lauren said. 'You look pretty disgusting yourself. I think it's your rat teeth. Or it might be your caterpillar eyebrows.'

I tried to laugh, but it stuck in my throat. 'I'm sorry,' I said. 'About being cross about bowling.'

'It doesn't matter. I should've just said yes.'

'But you weren't well enough, were you?'

She tensed. 'I was just tired.'

'It's more than that though, isn't it?'

'No.' She said it forcefully. 'I'm just run down. It's this time of year: everybody gets sick.'

'But you've been sick for months.'

She pushed herself more upright. 'I've only had a few days off school.'

'It's more than a few. All those days you said you were going to the orthodontist . . .'

Her eyes widened and I could tell that I'd struck on the truth.

'There was nothing wrong with your brace, was there?' My voice was getting louder.

She looked away. A horrible thought occurred to me.

'Oh my God, you didn't really go away for half-term, did you?'

She sucked in a breath. She'd lied to me; she'd lied so much. But then tears started rolling down her face and the red–hot anger inside of me just turned to icy fear. 'Why did you lie to me, Loz?' I could hardly get the words out.

She looked up at me. 'I didn't mean to.' She gulped. 'I don't know what's wrong with me. Ever since the glandular fever, I've been so tired and sometimes I think I'm all right and I go out and do something and then I feel so exhausted again that I can't even get out of bed.'

I sat down beside her. 'Why didn't you say?'

'I did in the beginning. But you got annoyed in the summer holidays when I was too tired to do things. You kept expecting me to have got over it.'

I felt my face getting warm. I remembered

dragging her to the lido when she'd said she didn't have the energy.

'And it's boring,' she went on. 'It's really boring always having to tell people you can't do things, or that you need to stop and rest, or that you can't even walk home from school. I just didn't want to talk about it any more.' She wiped away more tears. 'And it's scary. I don't know what's happening. I try not to think about it.'

'Have you been to the doctor?'

Lauren rolled her eyes. 'I'm practically living at the doctor's.'

My mouth was dry. 'What do they say is the matter with you?'

'First, they said it was the after-effects of the glandular fever, then they said I was anaemic and then they said I was depressed.' She slumped back on to her pillows. 'Basically, they haven't got a clue.'

We were quiet for a moment. I was relieved that she wasn't dying, but I could see how horrible it must be not knowing exactly what the problem was.

'I wish you'd talked to me about it,' I said.

'We've got better things to talk about.'

'Lauren, I'm your friend. I'm not just your friend when we're having a laugh and talking about Cute

Josh. I'm your friend when bad things happen too. I'm kind of hurt that you didn't tell me about any of this.'

'I'm sorry.' Her voice wobbled. 'I just kept hoping it would go away and it's not very . . . nice.'

'I'm always here. For the not-nice stuff too. Especially for the not-nice stuff.'

She gave me a watery smile. 'Thanks, Amelia.'

I gave her a hug. 'So what happens now? Is there something the doctors can do?'

'I'm having tests. Mostly they just say I need to take it easy. My mum's been talking to Iron Hair about me going part time at school.'

My heart plummeted, but I pulled my mouth into a smile. 'Well, that's something. The best way to attend school is not very often.'

She couldn't return the smile. It's funny how, even though we both say that we hate school, not being able to go is kind of a big deal. I squeezed her hand. 'Don't worry,' I said. 'It's not forever. You'll be better soon and then you'll be back in the madhouse full time with the rest of us.'

She nodded, but I could tell that she didn't believe it.

We only got to chat for a few minutes more before Lauren's mum appeared at the door and said, 'I think Lauren needs to rest now, Amelia.'

Lauren really did look shattered so I gave her a hug and said goodbye.

Mrs Anderson closed Lauren's door behind us and I followed her down the stairs in silence. At the bottom, she turned round to face me.

'Lauren tells me that she hasn't been entirely honest about her illness with you.'

Even though I wouldn't have said anything myself, I was glad that Lauren had because I didn't want her mum thinking I was a horrible friend.

'I didn't know she was so ill,' I said. 'And I honestly never meant to upset her.'

'I'm sorry if I was a bit short with you the other day. I thought that Lauren had explained things to you.'

'That's OK,' I said, even though it wasn't a particularly warm apology.

'Lauren *is* ill,' she said as if she needed to keep repeating it in case I was too stupid to understand. 'She has very limited reserves of energy, which means she tires easily. I'd be grateful if you could do your utmost to avoid wearing Lauren out.'

'Of course,' I said. 'I'll keep an eye on her.'

And she opened the door for me to leave.

I couldn't help feeling that she still wasn't that keen on me.

CHAPTER ❀ FIFTEEN

I was looking forward to Mum getting home from work on Monday night so that I could talk to her about Lauren. But, as usual, my house was complete madness until we'd all got in from school and sorted out tea. So I waited until after we'd eaten and I'd reminded Chloe it was her turn to supervise Lucy doing the washing-up.

'I don't need supervising,' Lucy complained. 'I'm already super.'

'Fine,' Chloe said, opening her wrestling magazine. 'I won't supervise you; I'll just watch you to make sure you do it right.'

'I don't need that either!'

Leaving them to it, I went to find Mum. She was standing in front of her wardrobe staring at the contents.

'Do you think these blouses make me look old?' she asked.

'You are old,' I answered.

Mum laughed. 'I know I seem ancient to you, but in the grand scheme of things forty is actually—'

'Very old.'

Mum shook her head. 'But do you think I should get some new outfits?'

I nearly said I didn't think it mattered because I didn't imagine anyone would notice, but it seemed like Mum was a bit bothered by her clothes all of a sudden, so I said, 'Yes, why don't you go shopping and get something that you really like?'

'Something youthful?'

'Why do you care about how wrinkly you look anyway? You're always telling us that it's what's inside that counts.'

Mum sat down on the bed. 'That's true. It's not that I really want to look young; it's more that I've realised that I haven't given much thought to my image for a long time. Most of these things I bought when I went back to work after Ella was born and that was over a decade ago.'

'Then you should get some new stuff. Is it to wear to work?'

'Maybe. I thought it'd be nice to have some casual things to wear out as well.'

'Out?'

'Mmm, you know, at the weekend or to my book club.'

Now I got it. Mum wanted some new clothes to impress her new friends at book club. 'You should definitely go shopping,' I said.

Mum nodded. 'Perhaps I will.'

It seemed to me that she was thinking about something other than just clothes, but before I could ask she said, 'Now what can I do for you? You look like you've got something on your mind.'

So I told her about Lauren.

'Oh dear,' she said when I'd finished. 'Poor Lauren. It's so hard to be struggling with your health.'

I thought that made Lauren sound like a pensioner who can't walk without one of those frames and wheezes every time they stand up. 'It's not that bad,' I said. 'Sometimes she's completely fine. And the doctors are doing tests on her so they can find out exactly what it is.'

'That's good. Just remember she might not be able to manage to do everything she did before. You'll have to be patient with her.'

'Of course I'll be patient with her!'

Mum patted my arm. 'I'm sure you will,

sweetheart. I'm just saying that things might be a bit different from before.'

Personally, I thought that things could only be better than they'd been for the last couple of months because at least now I knew what was going on. If Lauren needed a rest or for me to carry her bag then she could actually tell me, and we wouldn't fall out because she was trying to hide how tired she felt and being weird. But I didn't get to say this to Mum because Chloe bellowed up the stairs, '*MUUUUUUUUUM!*'

'What is it?' Mum called back in a normal voice, which is actually all it takes to be heard between upstairs and downstairs.

'There's a man on the phone who wants to interview me about that letter Suvi helped me write to the paper about what pigs they're being at the rugby club, but he says he has to talk to you first in case he's dodgy and a kidnapper. I told him that I could tell he wasn't a kidnapper because a kidnapper wouldn't say he wanted to talk to you, but he says he still has to talk to you and you have to be there when he interviews me, but it can be all my words. But he says they probably won't call the rugby club pigs. Can you come down?'

'Coming!' Mum called, rolling her eyes. She stood up and smiled at me. 'You girls are always up to something! Give Lauren my love and remember we can talk about this again later if you like.'

The journalist came round the next day after school. Mum got home as soon as school finished so that she could be there with Chloe.

I made sure that I opened the door to him.

'Jonathan Wellbeck, from *The Echo*,' he said. 'I'm here to interview Chloe.'

'There's not much chance that you'll want to kidnap her,' I said, stepping back to let him in. 'And, even if you did, you wouldn't be able to lift her.'

He gave a weak smile.

'Have you brought anyone to look after you?' I asked.

'Just me!' He laughed nervously.

'Well, if she offers to show you any wrestling moves, just say no. And check your watch is still on your wrist before you leave.'

I had planned to say a few more things to him. When you're trying to cut back on making smart remarks to your family, you have to get your fun somewhere, but the doorbell rang again, so I showed him into the kitchen where Mum and Chloe were waiting and went back to the door.

It was Ella. She'd stayed behind at school for

some super-boring tutor captain thing. 'Hi,' she said. 'Is he here?'

'Just arrived. They're doing the interview in the kitchen.'

'Oh,' Ella said in a whisper, as if us chatting in the hallway might disturb them. 'Do you think he'll print what Chloe wants him to?'

'He will if he knows what's good for him.'

Ella hung up her coat and scarf. 'Amelia, can I ask you something?'

'OK.'

'Crystal asked me to go to her house again.'

'So?'

'Do you think I should go?'

'Do you want to?'

Ella sat down on the bottom step of the stairs. 'I do because Crystal is fun, but I don't want to watch her be rude to her mum.'

'Ohhhhh, that. It was probably a one-off. What do Ashandra and Kayleigh think of this girl?'

'They like her. Kayleigh thinks I'm really lucky to get invited over. She says Crystal's house is like a footballer's place. There's the cinema and she's got a games room with table football and her bedroom is all matching pale blue and in their sitting room there's a ginormous white fluffy rug.'

I raised my eyebrows. 'Can you imagine a white fluffy rug in this house?'

Ella looked at me and we both laughed. Five minutes of being stroked by Lucy's grubby hands and being trodden on by Chloe's muddy trainers and any white rug would not be white any longer.

Ella stopped laughing. 'But I shouldn't really be thinking about her house, should I? I'm supposed to be pleased about seeing Crystal, not her table-football game.'

'You like Crystal, don't you?'

'Yes, she's really nice to me; she's helped me and Kayleigh loads with hockey.'

'Then it's fine. You're not supposed to like people just because they've got a big house but if you like someone first, and it turns out that they've got a cool house, then that's just lucky. As long as you don't stop liking her if she has to move into a shed.'

'I wouldn't.'

'Then enjoy your table football.'

CHAPTER ✦ SIXTEEN

The next day, when we got to Dad's house, Ella took one look at Suvi and said, 'Is Kirsti still not sleeping well?'

Suvi shook her head. We followed her into the kitchen where Lucy was bouncing a grizzly Kirsti in her bouncy chair. 'I don't mind her waking up in the night,' Suvi said. 'I know that all babies do this, but when she's had her feed she doesn't want to go back to sleep. I sing to her and rock her and tell her stories, but still she does not want to sleep.'

There was a pause because nobody knew anything helpful to say. 'I'm sure she'll get the hang of it soon,' Ella said eventually.

Suvi sighed. She plopped down on a chair and rested her elbows on the table, which was covered in thick books with glossy covers.

'What are you reading?' Chloe asked.

'Books about babies,' Lucy said, poking one with her finger. 'Why are you reading about babies?' she asked Suvi. 'We've got a real one.' She frowned at the photo of a chubby baby on the front of one of the books. 'Kirsti's better than this one. This one looks like he's got a poo in his nappy.'

'I remember your pooey nappies,' Chloe said to Lucy.

'I'm reading to find out about sleep patterns,' Suvi said quickly to stop Lucy yelling at Chloe. I don't think Chloe was even trying to wind Lucy up. She genuinely finds poo a fascinating subject. But Lucy hates being reminded that she was ever a baby.

'The amazing thing about books,' Suvi pressed on, 'is that they can help you with anything. Anything you want to do – get a baby to sleep, learn to speak Japanese or climb up a mountain – someone has done it before and you can read about it in a book.'

We all thought about that. I wondered if anyone had ever written a book about having a best friend with a tiredness problem.

'Is there a book about how to escape from a snake prison?' Lucy asked.

'Probably,' Suvi said.

'Is this whole book just about sleeping?' Chloe asked, picking one up. 'I could write a quicker one than that. You just close your eyes. Sleeping is easy.'

'I used to think that too,' Suvi said. And she buried her head in her baby instruction books again.

I left her to it and went upstairs to start on my history homework. At least I meant to start on my history, but I may have got a bit bored with that and ended up lying on my bed rereading *Flambards*.

Lucy came in and stood in front of me with her hands on her hips.

'Have you seen my secret book?' she asked.

'What does it look like?'

'I'm not telling; it's secret.'

I put down my book and pulled a face at her. 'How can I tell you if I've seen it if I don't know what it looks like?'

'You just remember all the books you've seen today and think if they could be my secret one.'

I picked up *Flambards* again. 'I haven't seen it.'

'You didn't do enough thinking! You have to help me!'

'When did you last have it?'

'A minute ago.'

'A minute ago? Then how can you have lost it? It can't have gone far.'

Because I was still trying to be less mean, I made Lucy retrace her steps and followed her round the house, looking for her stupid book. I need to find a way to be kind while still sitting down.

In the bathroom, the hand towel was on the floor in a heap. When I picked it up, there was Lucy's special book underneath. It was a notebook with owls printed on and across the front Lucy had written:

LUCY'S FRENDS BOOK.
PRIVUT.

'Here it is,' I said.

She snatched it out of my hands. 'Don't look! Why are you looking?'

'I'm looking because that's what you asked me to do. You asked me to find your book and, since I'm not a sniffer dog, I had to do that with my eyes. What are you writing about your friends anyway?'

She shoved the notebook up her jumper. 'You didn't see anything,' she said, like a tiny, menacing gangster.

I laughed, which she seemed to think meant I wasn't going to comply. I don't know why my family always think that me laughing means I'm going to cause trouble.

'I'll give you a lollipop to keep quiet,' she said and she slid a red lolly in a clear plastic wrapper out of her pocket.

'Where did you get that?' I asked.

'Don't worry; I've got more.'

'I wasn't actually fretting about whether you'd manage to hit your usual excessive levels of sugar; I was wondering why you've always got sweets these days.'

Lucy's eyes slid sideways. 'My friends give them to me.'

'Is this something to do with your book?'

Lucy gave a dramatic sigh. 'If you really want to know, they give me things because they want to get points in my book.'

'So you're saying your poor deluded friends are coughing up their sweets just so you'll give them a good score in your special book?' I said, realising that I'd discovered Lucy's scheme for getting her friends to do what she wanted.

Lucy attempted what I think she thought was a shy smile at her own brilliance. She looked like a baby crocodile. I've got to admit though, I was a tiny bit impressed.

'Basically, you're bribing your friends to be nice to you,' I said.

'Not really.'

'Yes you are. You're saying if they give you things and make a fuss of you, they'll get something from you.'

'But I don't actually have to give them anything. All I have to do is threaten them.'

'Well, that's just lovely. Don't you want people to be nice to you just because they like you?'

'Of course they like me. I just have to teach them the best way to make me happy.'

I gave her a hard stare. 'If you were my friend,' I said, 'I'd shove that lollipop up your nose.'

CHAPTER ❦ SEVENTEEN

Mr Garcia called Bartek and me up first at rehearsal. We started working through our song with Mr Garcia stopping us every other second to explain to us, in a lot of detail, what a horrible mess we were making of it. Actually, I thought we weren't too bad for a first go. Olivia was right about Bartek: he's got a great voice.

After Mr Garcia had delivered his millionth criticism and turned back to his music, Bartek crossed his eyes at me.

'Watch out for your hair,' I whispered.

But, even though Mr Garcia was all scowls and crashing chords on the piano to start with, we must have been making some improvement because eventually he said, 'I'm starting to think this might not be a complete disaster.' Which is as close to a compliment as Mr Garcia ever gets, so I was happy and Bartek was too because he gave me a high five.

While Mr Garcia was packing up, Bartek said, 'You're not so bad at singing.'

'You're not so bad yourself.'

'Hardly bad at all.' He was smirking. 'Only a little bit disgusting.'

'Oh yeah?' I said. 'And you're barely revolting and just a smidge horrendous.'

His eyes flashed and I knew he was enjoying himself. 'Your singing, it's only this much ...' He held his fingers a few centimetres apart. 'Only this much that it makes me want to be sick.'

'And your singing has only made my ears bleed the merest few drops.'

We kept on exchanging insults until we said goodbye at the gates. Bartek is really quite funny.

It was pouring with rain so I put up my hood and set off for Lauren's; by the time I got to her house, I was drenched and the plastic bag holding the magazines and chocolate I'd bought her was cutting into my hand, but I was looking forward to seeing her.

Mrs Anderson even managed a not entirely frosty 'Hello, Amelia' when she let me in.

Up in her room, Lauren was dressed and sitting on the floor, looking at our biology textbook.

'Hey,' I said. 'You look much better!'

'Thanks,' she said. Then she sighed and I felt like I'd said something dumb, even though she really did look much healthier. I stared out of the window. I always used to feel completely relaxed around Lauren, but now I was worrying about saying the wrong thing. There was a pause and then I handed her the bag of treats I'd brought.

'Oh, that's really sweet,' she said and put them on her bedside table without really looking at them. 'Are you going to sit down?'

I perched next to her and smoothed out the pleats on my skirt.

'Listen, Amelia . . .'

I looked up; she sounded serious.

'I went to the doctor's again this morning.'

A chill went through me. All my fears about a fatal condition came flooding back.

'What did they say?' I could hardly get the words out, my mouth was so dry.

'The doctor said he might know what's wrong with me.'

I swallowed. 'What is it?'

'It's this thing called Chronic Fatigue Syndrome.'

I was so relieved that she hadn't said any of the terrible illnesses I'd been thinking of that I felt my whole body sag. I had no idea what Chronic

Fatigue Syndrome was but it didn't sound too awful. 'Fatigue is just tiredness, isn't it?' I asked.

'Yeah. It basically means I'm tired all the time.'

I knew that already. 'So did he tell you when you'll be better? Do you have to take medicine?'

'He gave me some pills to take.' She didn't exactly sound cheerful about it.

'That's good, isn't it? When are you coming back to school?'

'I don't know. I am actually feeling a bit better at the moment.'

'Fantastic. Because Mr Champion has decided that he can't rest until we all know the many fascinating ways of joining two bits of wood together and I need you there to share in the good times.'

She smiled. 'Can't wait for that. How was rehearsal?'

'Mr Garcia said that if Bartek and I start using the brains and the lungs nature gave us there's a glimmer of hope that we might not entirely embarrass ourselves at the concert.'

'Wow. That's practically a hug coming from him. You two must be his favourites.'

'Bartek said that if Mr Garcia starts using his lungs we'd better all take shelter because his shouting will blow our heads off.'

'That's pretty funny.'

'He is funny. You'd like him. And he's so upbeat. He always makes rehearsals fun.' I couldn't help adding, 'I wish you were there.'

'Me too.' She looked sad and I felt like an idiot because I was supposed to be cheering her up.

'There's always the spring concert next term,' I said.

'Yeah, maybe.'

There was another pause. I'd never had to think this hard about what to say to Lauren before.

'So . . .' I started. I was going to tell her about what Iron Hair had said to Jasveen when she saw her running in the corridor, but then I thought that maybe I ought to be asking more about what was going on with Lauren. 'Did the doctor tell you what the recovery time is from this syndrome thing?'

Lauren stood up and threw herself on to the bed. 'Never mind all that stuff. Tell me what Cute Josh has been doing.'

In the end, we had a really good chat about almost everything except Lauren's health. I told her about Mr Champion's toxic new aftershave and how Cute Josh had worn his hair parted on the other side, and she showed me the bracelet her dad had sent her from his latest business trip. Lauren's mum didn't interrupt us or tell me it was time to go, even though I stayed until eight thirty.

That night, I went to bed feeling happy. Lauren wasn't dying. She had a diagnosis now and some pills to help her. I was doing quite well at being less snappy with people. Singing with Bartek was good fun and our duet was coming along nicely. All I wanted was for Lauren to come back to school and then everything would be perfect.

CHAPTER ❤ EIGHTEEN

Usually, Saturday is my favourite day of the week, but recently, without Lauren to hang out with, they've all been a bit of a disappointment. By half past ten, Lucy was back from her ballet lesson and practising flying leaps in the Pit because she was hoping to get them high enough to knock Madame Donna's glasses off next week. Ella had gone to the fabulous Crystal's house and Chloe was kicking a ball about in the garden. Mum was planning lessons at the table in the sitting room and I was slumped on the sofa. I was the only one without anything to do. Fantastic.

'I am so bored,' I sighed.

'I'm sorry to hear that, love,' Mum said. 'Why don't you visit Lauren?'

'I rang. Her mum says she's resting and then she's got to do some schoolwork.'

'Can't you go out with your other friends?'

'Milly and Jasveen have gone to London for the day. I tried Olivia and Bethany, but they're not answering their phones. They're probably doing something together because they're best friends. Everybody is in pairs, and even when they let me tag along, my best friend is missing and it isn't the same.'

'If it's any consolation, I'm a bit fed up too. Shall we make some cookies?'

I looked at Mum. I mean, properly looked at her. Most of the time you don't really see your own mum because you think you know what she looks like and your eyes just kind of skim over her. She didn't look great, but I've seen her look worse. Last half-term, when her school was being inspected, she was exhausted all of the time; now she looked more ... droopy. Her hair was all flat and her skin was pale and she just seemed washed out.

Mum started stacking up her books and gave me a wink. Even though she was down, she was trying to make me feel better. My brain started whirling around, thinking about Mum. I've got to admit that I'm not very good at thinking about other people. For a long time after the divorce, I was upset, and the problem with feeling angry and hurt inside is that it takes up a lot of your thinking. You're so mad about the way you feel that you don't notice how anybody else is feeling. And, even though I made up with Dad before half-term and decided that I wouldn't be so mean and selfish any more, thinking only about yourself is a really bad habit to get into because it's quite hard to stop. But looking at Mum, all pale and limp, I stopped worrying about my day and instead I saw a way that I could make hers much better, even if it wasn't going to be very much fun for me.

'Mum,' I said. 'I think you should go out for the day. Why don't you ring Susan?'

Mum blinked in surprise. 'Well, I suppose we could all go shopping or maybe swimming. Would you like that?'

'Never mind me; you should go out just the two of you with no annoying kids interrupting.'

'I don't know, love. I don't like leaving you girls.'

'I told you before; I'm old enough to be in charge.'

She didn't look so sure.

'I won't let them get up to anything,' I said. 'No breaking stuff or painting stuff or jumping on stuff.'

She smiled. 'And no using the drill?'

'I won't let Lucy anywhere near it.'

'I suppose it is daytime.'

'Yep. And we all know that burglars and kidnappers only come out at night.'

I regretted joking because her smile disappeared. 'Perhaps I'd better not.'

'You definitely should; you deserve a day out.'

She thought about it. 'You haven't even got Ella here to help ... But I suppose, if you promise not to let Lucy out, not any further than the garden ...'

'I promise.'

'We were talking about our book group going for coffee sometime. Maybe I could see if anyone is free then we could just go to that place down the road.'

So Mum made some phone calls and arranged to meet Susan and two other book club people at the café, then she hopped in the shower and put on her favourite flowery dress. By the time she kissed us goodbye, her hair was bouncing around her face and her eyes were bright and she looked much happier.

When I closed the door behind her, I realised that I was smiling too. The thing about doing something horrible, like keeping Chloe and Lucy out of trouble when you should be enjoying your Saturday so that Mum can have a nice time, is that it does make you feel good.

In the kitchen, Lucy shrieked.

But you do still have to get through the horrible bit.

*

After I'd combed all the soggy Weetabix out of Lucy's hair, and told Chloe that she wasn't allowed to pelt Lucy with mushed-up cereal even if Lucy did call her Lumpy Bum, there wasn't any more trouble. Chloe went back to ball-kicking in the garden and when I went to check on Lucy she was curled up on the broken sofa in the Pit and hunched over her notebook, scribbling away.

'Is that your friends book?' I asked.

'Nope.'

'So what are you writing?' I asked.

'Nothing,' she said, scratching the pen furiously across the page like she was underlining something.

'Who's the top scorer then?' I asked.

She looked up at me with what I think she imagines is a chilling stare. 'You don't have the security clearance for me to share that information with you.'

'Fine.' I backed out of the room.

Mum should never have let her watch James Bond.

CHAPTER ❤ NINETEEN

Mum seemed really pepped up by her time out. The next morning, I found her making sandwiches in the kitchen.

'We're going to the beach for a picnic,' she said.

'Isn't it a bit cold for that?' I asked.

'Nonsense! The sun's out today. Anyway, it will be invigorating; a brisk walk along the front and then I promise we'll go and play in the arcade on the pier.'

I do quite like going to the arcade. They've got this great shooting game where you have to team up with the vampires to kill all the zombies. Me and Chloe are on the top scorers list.

'Unless you've got other plans?' Mum asked.

'Nope. Absolutely nothing.'

Chloe appeared in the doorway.

'What about you, Chloe? Do you want to come to the beach or are you going out with Thunder?'

Chloe pulled a face. 'I'm not that keen on Thunder at the moment.'

Mum put down the butter knife. 'That's a bit unfair, isn't it? It's not his fault they won't let girls on the youth squad.'

'I know it's not! But I can't help it; whenever I see him, he talks about rugby and it makes me cross, so I'm just . . . avoiding him a bit.'

'Come and sit down, sweetheart,' Mum said, pulling out a chair for Chloe and another one for herself.

Chloe sighed and sat down.

'I've been thinking about you and Thunder. Because you remind me of myself and Imogen.'

'Really? I hope I'm you because Imogen has got hair coming out of her ears.'

'Actually, you are me because I think we've both had to struggle with the same problem with our friends.'

'What problem?'

'Well, you know that Imogen and I have been friends for a long time? Ever since we first started teaching, we've been mates. We don't see each other so much since we moved out of London, but we used to spend a lot of time together.'

'And?' Chloe asked.

'We both got married at around the same time and we were both really looking forward to having children. But although it seemed like all of our friends were getting pregnant it didn't happen for me and Imogen.'

'I didn't know that,' I said.

Mum smiled at me. 'I've never mentioned it before; it seems incredible now that I've got you lovely lot, but for a year or two I worried that I would never have a baby.'

'But then you did,' Chloe said.

'Ah, but before that Imogen got pregnant.'

'Did you feel bad?' Chloe asked.

'I did.'

'So I bet it was hard being around her,' Chloe said. 'Did you avoid her?'

'It was certainly tempting. The thing is that we all know how important it is to look after your friends and be there when things are tough for them, but it's important to share their good times too. If you care about your friends then you need to show them friendship when times are hard *and* you need to be happy for them when they get the things they want. Even if that thing is what you desperately want for yourself.'

Chloe flopped forward. 'I know I'm supposed

to be happy for Thunder, but I'm not. I'm just not. It's not fair.'

'I think you're mixing up how you feel about what's happened to you and what's happened to Thunder. They're two different things. You're allowed to be sad that you've missed out on joining a rugby squad, but that shouldn't stop you from being pleased for Thunder. You want Thunder to do well and be happy, don't you?'

Chloe propped herself up on her elbows. 'Yes, but ... you're making it sound easy. Maybe it should be different things, but it isn't separate inside me; it's all mixed up like when Lucy swirls her shepherd's pie together. I keep trying to be pleased for him, but I'm not.'

'Then sometimes you have to do what I did at Imogen's baby shower. You pretend. You take all the friendship and love you have for that person and you use it to cover up how bad you're feeling and you say, "Congratulations!" And sometimes, if you're lucky, saying that will help you to really feel it.'

'Do you think Imogen knew how you felt?' I asked.

'I expect she had an idea. And I think she appreciated the fact that I didn't push her away or tell her it wasn't fair. Sometimes being a really good friend is as much about what you manage not to say as what you do say.'

I could see Chloe was mulling this over. 'So you're saying I have to say well done to Thunder?'

'You don't have to do anything. Just remember that Thunder hasn't got on to the squad to hurt you.'

'OK, I'll think about that.' She stood up. 'And Mum?'

'What, love?'

'When we get to the beach, am I allowed to go paddling?'

CHAPTER ☙ TWENTY

Monday lunchtime, I was walking across the cafeteria when I spotted Chloe with Thunder. Thunder was clearly in the middle of telling a story. He was on his feet, miming throwing a rugby ball. As I got closer, I heard Chloe say, 'That's awesome. They're definitely going to pick you for the match team.'

She sounded happy, but when I looked at Chloe's face I could see that, even though her mouth was smiling, her eyes weren't. She was really trying to be pleased for Thunder, just like Mum had said. As I walked past, I gave her a squeeze on the shoulder. She looked up and smiled, a real smile, but there wasn't time to say anything because the bell rang and I had to get to my next lesson.

I wasn't much looking forward to physics

without Lauren again but, just after I'd sat down, Bartek came up to me and said, 'Can I sit here?'

'OK,' I said.

He grinned at me and I smiled back, but then I had to pretend to look for something in my pencil case because I was worried that I was blushing, which was silly because what on earth was there to blush about?

We didn't actually get to chat much because Mrs Padley is pretty strict, but Bartek did show me a cartoon he'd drawn of Mr Garcia with steam coming out of his ears. He's nearly as good at drawing as he is at singing.

At the end of the lesson, he said, 'I'm looking forward to singing with you at rehearsal.'

And I realised I was looking forward to it too.

When Mum and Lucy got home that evening, Lucy was unusually quiet. She didn't jump on anything or shout at anyone; she just sat on the sofa with the corners of her mouth turned down.

'Are you OK?' Ella asked her.

Lucy didn't answer.

Personally, I think that when Lucy decides to keep her mouth shut we should all just be grateful for the peace and quiet, but Ella seemed dead set on getting her to talk.

'Do you want a biscuit?' Ella asked.

Lucy shook her head.

'What would you like?'

I could see the struggle on Lucy's face; she was obviously determined to keep her silence up, but she couldn't resist the offer of whatever she wanted. I wondered what Ella would do if Lucy said she'd like a puppy.

Lucy opened her mouth, paused till she was sure she had mine and Ella's full attention and then announced, 'I want to be a bat.'

It's not just hedgehogs and rabbits that Lucy likes. She's also very fond of bats and her idea of having a good time is hanging upside down on the climbing frame in the skatepark down the road, pretending to be a bat.

'Will one of you take me?' Lucy asked, fluttering her eyelids in what I think she imagines is an appealing way, but really just makes her look like she's got something in her eye.

I waited. If you wait long enough, someone else will always volunteer.

Ella sighed. 'I could take you quickly, but I have got a lot of homework to do.'

'I suppose I could go,' I found myself saying.

'Why don't you both go?' Mum said from the hall. 'That way you'll have someone to talk to while Lucy is getting battish. Tea will be on the table in twenty minutes anyway.'

So we put on our coats and went down the road to the skatepark.

Lucy swung into position on the climbing frame and wriggled with pleasure. Weird.

'Do you feel better now?' Ella asked her.

'Yes,' Lucy said. 'Because bats don't have rubbish friends that say their secret friends book is stupid.'

'Maybe that's because they're not silly enough to have a secret friends book in the first place,' I said.

Lucy put her fingers in her ears and swung about a bit. Ella and I stood shoulder to shoulder for warmth.

'You never told me what you did at Princess Crystal's house on Saturday,' I said. I'd asked her twice, but she'd managed to change the subject both times.

Ella rubbed at the ground with the toe of her boot. 'We played table football and made cupcakes.'

'Wow, don't tell Chloe! If you throw in some wrestling and a farting competition, that's her idea of heaven.'

Ella didn't look like she'd had a heavenly time.

'Was Crystal a brat again?'

Ella rubbed her mittened hands together. 'She's nice to me,' she said. 'She let me choose what kind of cupcakes to make and she said I was the best at icing.'

'What's the problem then?'

Ella looked like she had a pain in her stomach; she hates criticising anyone. 'I just think she's a bit rude. The lady who cleans her house was doing the hoovering in the games room when we wanted to play in there and Crystal said, "You'll have to do that later," to her like she was a servant or something.'

Frankly, I was just amazed by the idea of anyone having someone else come to clean their house and I wondered if I could convince Mum that a cleaner was a good way to spend her money, but I tried to focus back on what Ella was saying. 'You know you don't have to go there, don't you?' I asked.

Ella didn't answer that. 'I talked to Kayleigh about it. She thinks that maybe Crystal will get better and not be so rude,' she said. 'Or maybe I'll stop minding.'

I didn't think either of those things was likely to happen, but I decided that Ella probably had to work that out for herself.

CHAPTER ♥ TWENTY-ONE

Wednesday morning is always a bit of a scramble because everybody has to remember to pack anything that they need to take to Dad's. Mum tells us to do it the night before, but only Ella is ever that organised.

I'd crammed everything I reckoned I needed into my bag and was trying to have a nice quiet pee, while everyone else was flapping, but before I could finish Chloe came barging into the bathroom.

'I'm famous!' she said triumphantly.

I was going to shoo her away, but being famous is probably just about important enough to interrupt my privacy for.

'She means she's in the newspaper,' Lucy explained, following her in, holding a copy of *The Echo*.

I tutted. That wasn't the kind of famous I was thinking of and now there were two of them just staring at me on the loo.

'Oh, come right on in, take a seat, why don't you?' I said.

Chloe sat down on the side of the bath. Seriously?

Once I'd pulled up my school trousers and washed my hands, I took the newspaper from Lucy and had a good look at the page she was pointing at.

'That is actually quite cool,' I admitted. Chloe was right there on page seven, with a photo of her holding a rugby ball and everything.

'And look! Did you see what it says? The rugby club have said that they're going to run girls' training too! Because of me!'

'That's fantastic!' And I have to admit that I did end up doing a little dance with Chloe right there in the bathroom.

'Does this mean Chloe's going to be on telly?' Lucy asked.

Chloe twirled in front of the mirror. 'I might be! I could be on the news like Thunder was.'

'Will you have to start wearing sunglasses and will those people with cameras follow you around and put you in a magazine with a picture of your knickers showing?' Lucy asked.

'I don't think that's going to happen,' Chloe said.

'Thank goodness,' I said. It's bad enough that Chloe flashes her knickers when she does cartwheels in the park. I'd die of embarrassment if her knickers made it into a gossip magazine.

'She's not really famous then,' Lucy insisted.

'Famous enough,' Chloe said, cutting out the article with Mum's nail scissors that are absolutely only ever to be used to cut nails.

'Well done, Clo,' I said and grabbed my face wash to put in my bag, but as I was running down the stairs a horrible thought hit me. My history essay was due tomorrow and I hadn't even started it.

I found Mum in the kitchen.

'Can I ring you tonight?' I asked. 'After your book club? Because I've got this history thing to do and Dad is rubbish at history.'

Mum wiped up the ring of milk and cornflakes Lucy had left around her cereal bowl. 'It'd be better if you could make it before book club.' She hesitated. 'I think I might be popping to the pub after we've finished.'

She turned to the sink so I couldn't see her face, but I was already convinced something was going on. 'Who are you going with?' I asked.

'Oh, just someone from the group.'

She sounded a little bit flustered. 'Mum! It's not a man, is it?'

She couldn't help laughing. 'It is a man, but there's nothing to get excited about. I just enjoy chatting to him. You don't mind, do you?'

I hated it when my dad started dating Suvi. Even if my parents didn't want to be together, I couldn't see why he needed a girlfriend. But I understand a bit better now. Grown-ups like grown-up company. And romance. I didn't much like the idea of Mum getting smoochy with someone, but if anyone deserved to be happy it was Mum, so I concentrated on saying something that was both true and nice, and I managed to come up with, 'I think it's a great idea for you to have some fun.'

Mum let out a sigh of relief; I guessed that maybe she'd been a bit worried about telling me and how I'd react, so I was pleased that I hadn't made a fuss.

'Don't mention it to your sisters just yet, will you?'

I nodded. I was pleased that Mum had told me an almost-secret; it felt as if she was treating me more like an adult.

'Anyway, I'll be around to discuss history until about six thirty.'

'Got it.'

'Or you could always ask Suvi to help with your homework.'

Even though I'd been getting on better with

Suvi, I still wasn't sure that would go well, so I chose to ignore that suggestion.

'I'd better get to school,' I said, scooping up my bag. 'I hope you have a nice time tonight.'

'Thank you, Amelia.'

'And remember,' I said over my shoulder. 'Don't stay out too late. You've got school in the morning, young lady.'

CHAPTER ✦ TWENTY-TWO

During dinner at Dad's house, I got a text message from Lauren saying she was coming back to school the next day. Even though Suvi is normally huffy about people having their phones at the table, someone must have told her about Lauren because when I read out the message she said, 'This is excellent,' and helped me to some more green beans, which I suppose, in her wholefood world, is the closest thing to a celebration.

The next morning, Dad was surprised to find me in the kitchen already spooning up my cereal when he came downstairs.

'I normally have to prise you out of bed,' he said. 'Getting you away from your duvet is like trying to peel two slices of processed cheese apart.'

I beamed at him. 'I'm giving you a day off from cheese-peeling.' Actually, for once, I was really looking forward to going to school because I'd be able to see Lauren.

Even though I left early, by the time I got to our tutor room, Lauren was already there.

'I'm so glad you're back!' I said, giving her a hug.

She laughed. 'I can't believe that I'm saying this, but I'm really glad to be here. Even though it's school, I really missed everybody.'

'Bet you didn't miss Mr Champion and his lessons.'

'Maybe I did. Maybe I secretly enjoy having someone with a ratty moustache tell me I'm an idiot while I try to operate a gigantic saw without chopping my fingers off.'

'You are quite weird so you probably do.'

'I'll tell you who I did miss,' she said in a low voice and jerked her head in the direction of the hallway.

Cute Josh and his friends were walking past our classroom.

Lauren and I tried to stare without looking like we were staring.

'He'll be in maths later,' I said. 'You should talk to him.'

Lauren gave me her sceptical face. 'Yeah, and you should tell Mr Champion that he smells of wet dog.'

We cracked up.

All morning we chatted and mucked about just like we always used to. It was brilliant.

During maths, Lauren really did speak to Cute Josh because he sat behind us and he asked if he could borrow the ruler she was using, which was actually my ruler so it's a shame it wasn't in my hand when he asked, but Lauren acted very cool and just handed it over. When he gave it back, he said, 'Thanks,' and Lauren said, 'That's all right.' When she turned back round in her seat, I silently pointed to the ruler. It must have been Lucy's because it had a bright pink My Little Pony sticker on it.

'CJ probably thinks you're a big fan,' I said under my breath.

We spent the rest of the lesson trying to stifle our giggles.

In drama, Lauren was very noble and didn't even mention the fact that she was stuck playing the maid, which is the tiniest part. Instead, she wrote some helpful notes about costumes for us all. The whole thing was coming together really well. I even had to admit that Milly was doing quite a good job as the mother.

'I definitely think that our group could be the best in the class,' I said to Lauren afterwards, when we were queuing for lunch.

She nodded. Other people might think I'm showing off when I say something like that, but Lauren knows that drama is my joint best subject and how much I want us to do well this term.

'I'll tell you what would be cool,' she said, sliding her tray along to the sandwich section. 'If Mrs Ling thought we were so good that she remembered us when it's time to cast the musical next year.'

In the summer, our school always does a big musical production, but you're only allowed to audition for a main part once you're in Year Nine, so this was our first year of having a chance at a leading role. It was so good to hear Lauren sounding enthusiastic about us getting involved in a school show again.

'I hope she does,' I said, putting my tray down on an empty table. 'We'd be awesome in one of the big parts.'

Lauren didn't answer because she was flopping down into a cafeteria chair.

'Are you OK?' I asked. 'Do you need some water?'

'I'm all right. I've got some, thanks.'

And she reached out for her bag.

'I can get it,' I said.

'It's fine.'

But she looked like all the colour had been drained out of her face.

'Shall I take you to the office?' I asked.

'No. I just need a drink.'

She gulped down some water and took a few deep breaths. It didn't make her look any less like a zombie.

'Are you sure you don't wa—'

'Amelia! You're starting to sound like my mum!'

That shut me up. Eventually, Lauren started eating her sandwich so I did the same. I felt like I'd put my foot in it, even though I'd only wanted to help.

'Sorry,' she said. 'I'd just rather talk about something else. Tell me about the other drama groups.'

So I wittered on about what they were doing and then, when I'd run out of steam on that topic, I moved on to Olivia's plans for a New Year's Eve party. But I barely even knew what I was saying because all the time I was thinking about the fact that we had PE next lesson and I didn't know how to tell Lauren that I really didn't think she was up to it.

'We'd better get moving,' I said eventually. 'Mrs Henderson seems to think that we all love PE so much that we should give up the last few minutes of lunch so that we're ready to run around like idiots the second the bell goes.'

'I'm not coming to PE,' Lauren said.

'Now I'll have to face the hockey balls and the scorn of the sporty girls all by myself,' I said, even though, really, I was relieved that Lauren wasn't going to try and run around the hockey pitch in her condition. 'Has your mum written you a note?'

'No, I'm going home. Remember I told you that Iron Hair arranged for me to do half-days because of, you know . . .' She looked away. 'My chronic fatigue.'

'Oh,' I said. Of course I knew that things were going to be a bit different, but I hadn't quite realised how different they'd be. 'So you're going home after lunch every day now?' I asked.

'Don't look like that! At least I got to be here for the morning. And my mum didn't even want me to stay for lunch but I managed to persuade her that it would fit in better with her shifts.'

I tried really hard to stop looking like 'that', even though I didn't know exactly what it was I'd been looking like. 'You're right,' I said. 'It's great that you get to stay for lunch.'

But really I was struggling to get my head around everything. I'd thought that now Lauren had a diagnosis things would get easier, and I'd know how best to support her, but I felt like I'd let her down twice in one lunch hour. I'd been too protective, yet I'd also underestimated how much Lauren's condition was going to affect her school life.

I tried to give Lauren my most reassuring smile. But I felt like an idiot.

CHAPTER ♥ TWENTY-THREE

Ella stayed after school on Friday for a tutor captain meeting, which meant I had someone to walk to Dad's with after my extra soloists' rehearsal. For an eleven-year-old, Ella is a surprisingly good person to chat with. Maybe it's because she lets me do most of the talking.

'How's Lauren?' Ella asked.

'Pretty good. She went home at lunchtime again. She missed maths.'

'That's a shame,' Ella said.

I hoped that she was talking about the fact that I only had half a day with Lauren rather than thinking it was a shame that she'd missed maths. But Ella is so maths-crazy that you never know. Although actually, Lauren probably will be sorry that she missed this lesson because Cute Josh asked me where she was. Which seemed to suggest that he liked Lauren enough to notice when she wasn't there. Although a tiny part of me was hoping that maybe he asked so that he'd have something to say to me.

'Did you have a good rehearsal?' Ella asked.

'Uh-huh. Mr Garcia said we'd made a few millimetres' progress since yesterday.'

'Mr Garcia covered our lesson when Mr O'Brien was away. He got really cross. Isn't it scary being alone with him?'

I shrugged. 'Not really. You shouldn't be so afraid of teachers, Ella; they can't eat you.'

'No, but they can shout and tell you that you've done it all wrong and ask what on earth were you thinking and then twitch their upper lip with rage.'

I laughed. 'That does pretty much sum up Mr Garcia.'

'Aren't you upset when he tells you you're messing it up?'

'No. I need to know when I'm making mistakes.'

'He could be a bit nicer about it.'

Actually, I prefer Mr Garcia's approach. I hate it when teachers don't tell people they're wrong and say things like 'Good try' when everyone knows it was a stupid answer. I like to know where I am. Mr Garcia doesn't muck about.

'His bark's worse than his bite,' I said.

Ella shuddered. 'I think you're very brave having rehearsals with him.'

'They're quite fun really and, whenever Mr Garcia says something mean, Bartek does an impression of him behind his back. You can't be scared when you're trying not to snort with laughter.' I was planning on getting Bartek to do one of his impressions for Lauren; she was going to love it. 'What was your meeting like?' I asked.

'It was very interesting. We've been thinking about how to make the school more energy efficient.'

'Scintillating.'

'Well, it is important. If the school sets a good example then we can encourage all the kids to be greener. I suggested that we organise a team t—' She broke off mid-sentence with a jerk of the head. 'Oh no!'

'What's the matter?' I asked.

'I've forgotten my swimming stuff.'

We were all supposed to be going swimming with Dad the next morning.

'I had it all ready in a bag by my bed and then Lucy knocked over the shampoo in the bathroom and I went to help her and I forgot all about it.'

'Never mind,' I said. 'Just give Mum a ring and she can drop it over.'

'But she's going to the cinema with her book group.' Ella looked at her watch. 'She'll need to leave soon if she's going to the early showing.'

'We can always get it tomorrow morning.'

'But it'll wake her up. She needs a lie-in.'

I looked at Ella. It must be quite tiring being the worrying type. She was completely worked up about her silly swimming stuff. 'Don't panic,' I said. 'It's not far out of our way and I've got my key.'

'So we can get it now? You don't mind?'

I shrugged.

'Thanks, Amelia!'

Ella's so funny. She looked genuinely relieved, as if not having her swimming things was a punishable offence. We backtracked a bit and cut across the park. When we got to our road, I could see a light on in the kitchen.

'I don't think she's left yet,' I said.

I let us in and called, 'Mum!'

She came out of the kitchen and into the hallway looking a bit flustered. 'Everything all right?' she asked. 'Why are you here and not at your dad's?'

'I forgot my swimming stuff an—' Ella began.

In the kitchen, there was the scrape of a chair as someone stood up.

'Who's here?' Ella asked.

159

I tried to look over Mum's shoulder into the kitchen.

Mum smiled. 'Just one of my friends from book group. Come and meet him.'

I followed Mum, but Ella didn't move. She never likes meeting people. I grabbed her hand. 'It's fine,' I whispered. 'We don't have to stay.' She let me pull her into the kitchen.

'Girls,' Mum said. 'This is Greg.'

I just knew this must be the man she went to the pub with. He was on his feet, putting his coffee cup in the sink. I guessed he was a little older than Mum; his hair was going grey at the sides and he had those creasy lines around his eyes. He was wearing a checked shirt and chinos. He looked OK. Like a teacher when you go on a school trip and they look a bit weird in their casual clothes.

'Hi,' I said.

'This is my eldest, Amelia,' Mum said.

'I'm the difficult one,' I said.

Mum tutted, but Greg laughed, which made me like him a bit more.

I nudged Ella, but she didn't say anything.

'And this is Ella,' I said. 'She's the quiet one.'

Greg laughed again.

'We just came back to get Ella's swimming things,' I explained. 'We're going swimming tomorrow.' Then I couldn't resist adding: 'With our dad.' I don't mind Mum making new friends but for some reason I wanted him to know that we have got a dad. And that he takes us swimming.

The wind whipped round the garden, sending a plastic flowerpot bowling across the patio. 'I hope it's an indoor pool!' Greg said.

I waited to see if Ella would say anything, but she didn't so I said, 'Yep. Nice and warm. And it's got slides. We'll probably have a hot chocolate afterwards, won't we, Ella?'

Ella just looked at me.

'Good idea,' Greg struggled on, but I could tell that he thought Ella was being weird. I thought she was being weird and she's my sister.

'Well,' said Mum, putting an arm round Ella, 'you'd better fetch your costume otherwise your dad and Suvi will be wondering where you've got to.'

Ella shuffled out of the room with her eyes on the floor.

'Do you want me to drop you over there?' Mum asked.

I shook my head. 'You don't need to. I'll ring Suvi and tell her we're on our way.' I looked up at the clock. 'Anyway, aren't you going to be late for your film?'

Mum reached for her bag. 'We should really be making a move. We're supposed to be meeting the others outside . . .'

'We'll be fine,' I insisted. 'We always walk to Dad's, remember?'

'Well, if you're sure.'

I took another sneaky look at Greg. He was studying our noticeboard and pretending not to listen. I wondered if he was cross with us for interrupting. He didn't seem the cross type. That was good. If Mum had to date then I really wanted it to be someone nice and kind who wouldn't scowl at us or frighten Ella. Mind you, despite the fact Greg looked like a geography teacher, Ella already did seem frightened. I heard her come back downstairs but she stopped in the middle of the hallway, clearly not planning on coming any closer.

'Nice to meet you, Greg,' I said. 'Enjoy the film. See you Monday, Mum.'

I had to take hold of Ella again to get her moving towards the door. Her face was pink.

'Bye, girls,' Mum said.

'Bye,' I said.

Ella made a faint noise that might have been a goodbye and I pulled her out of the door.

'What's the matter?' I asked as soon as we got to the end of the driveway.

'Nothing,' she said.

'Ella, as soon as you saw that man, you froze like an icicle. Did you really feel that shy?'

She looked down at the ground and then at the sky. 'Maybe. I do get shy.'

'I know, but you usually manage a hello. I hope Greg doesn't think you were rude.' Then she looked so upset that Mum's check-shirted boyfriend might think she had no manners that I said, 'It doesn't matter; I don't think he even noticed. He was too busy making kissy faces at Mum.'

Ella looked like she might faint. 'He wasn't, was he?'

Suddenly I missed Lauren. When I say outrageous things to her, she says something outrageous right back. Ella is way too sensitive for my sense of humour. 'No,' I admitted. 'He didn't. Don't worry about it.'

But, even though she didn't say anything more about it, I'm not sure she took my advice.

CHAPTER ♥ TWENTY-FOUR

Dad woke us up crazy early to go swimming. I'm not kidding: it was still dark. I'm not a big fan of early mornings, especially at the weekend, but I dragged myself out of bed and into some clothes. When we got to the pool, I had to admit that it was worth the effort because we were almost the only people there. We didn't have to queue for the slides or share the wave pool or anything.

Eventually, Dad said that we'd better get going or Lucy would be late for ballet, so we headed for the changing rooms.

'Are you going straight to rugby?' I asked Chloe.

'Yep,' she grinned. 'And it's going to be awesome.'

'What about you, Ella?' I asked quickly, not wanting Chloe to get stuck on the subject of rugby. Ever since someone important at the rugby club rang her personally to say that they hoped she'd be signing up for the girls' training sessions, she'd hardly spoken about anything else.

'I'm going to the cinema with Crystal and Kayleigh and Ashandra later,' Ella said.

I squeezed the water out of my hair. 'Really? I thought after last time you wouldn't want to spend any more time with Crystal.'

'I just don't want to go to her house because I don't like being there when she's horrible to her mum. The cinema will be fine. Ash and Kay will be there anyway.'

I told Dad I was going to Lauren's house and that I'd walk because I knew her mum insisted that she got extra sleep at the weekends and I thought if I strolled there slowly she'd have had plenty of time for a lie-in. But when I knocked on Lauren's door and her mum opened it she said, 'Oh, I'm sorry, Amelia, Lauren's not here.'

Which doesn't sound like a particularly crazy thing for someone's mum to say but for such a long time Lauren has only been at home (or school) so I couldn't quite believe that she wasn't there. I was pretty sure she hadn't been anywhere since we went to the milkshake bar weeks ago. It seemed impossible that she could be out. Anybody else's mum might have told me where she was. But Mrs Anderson didn't say and I couldn't bring myself to ask. In fact, she was clearly waiting for me to push off. 'You hadn't made plans, had you?' she asked.

'No.' I'd not even thought to ring Lauren to say I was coming because I'd just assumed she'd be in. 'No, it's OK, I'll call her later.'

I didn't know what to do with myself then. I thought about ringing Lauren now, but she obviously wasn't interested in seeing me, otherwise she'd have let me know that she was up to going out today. So I rang Jasveen instead. She and Milly were in town so I decided to go and hang out with them.

I caught the bus and took a seat at the front. I tried to put Lauren out of my mind, but I couldn't help wondering where she was. I'd just managed to focus on what I was going to wear for the Christmas concert when, out of the window, I saw Lauren. She was sitting on the low wall that boys lean their bikes against outside KFC. Cute Josh was sitting next to her. My jaw dropped open. I turned my head to watch them as the bus sped past. What on earth? Why was Lauren with Josh? Was it a date? Did her mum know about this? Why didn't I know about this?

By the time I got off the bus, I was still in a daze.

The image of the pair of them flashed into my mind. Lauren hadn't looked tired at all. In fact, she'd been laughing. So had Josh. She hadn't been to my house in ages, and couldn't last a whole day at school, but now suddenly she had the energy to walk all the way to KFC and roll about laughing with Josh?

I don't think going round the shops with me was much fun for Jasveen and Milly. I didn't say much and every time one of them mentioned Lauren's name I flinched. In the end, I just left them to it.

When I got back to Dad's house, Chloe was blocking the hallway and talking excitedly to Ella.

'Where's Dad?' I asked Ella.

'He and Suvi have taken Lucy and Kirsti to the supermarket; they'll be back soon.'

'Are you all right?' Chloe asked.

'Fine. Stop staring at me.'

'You look a bit funny.'

I wasn't in the mood for Chloe's smart remarks. 'You're the one covered in mud.'

'I've just had rugby. Remember? It was my first session today.'

'Oh yeah, I can't think how that slipped my mind. I ringed it on my calendar and everything.'

'It was amazing.'

She had hair sticking up all over the place, a dirt smudge across her cheek and it was obvious that she'd been worked pretty hard because she had clearly visible sweat rings on the pale blue rugby shirt she was wearing.

'Is that the team shirt?' Ella asked. Chloe had gone on and on about how Thunder and the other youth squad members had been given swish shirts with their names printed on the back.

Chloe shook her head. 'They didn't give us shirts. This is an old one of Thunder's; he grew out of it.'

Ella and I stared at the shirt. It was gigantic.

'Well, you look like a proper rugby player,' Ella said.

'Uh-huh and you smell like one too,' I added.

'What was the stadium like?' Ella asked quickly.

Chloe's face fell. 'It wasn't at the stadium; the girls are going to do their training at Langley Fields.'

'Oh,' Ella said.

I couldn't be bothered with this. I sat down at the bottom of the stairs and started unlacing my boots. 'Does it matter where you are?' I snapped. 'As long as you all get to roll around in the mud and end up smelling like overweight warthogs on a hot day. That's the point of it, isn't it?'

Chloe glared at me. 'The point is rugby.'

'And what was that like?' Ella asked in an annoyingly sweet voice.

Chloe stopped glaring. 'Well, actually, that was really good. We did some throwing and kicking drills and they said that one week we might go and watch a women's match.'

I trudged upstairs towards our room. I needed to be alone to try and think about Lauren and what was going on with her.

Chloe followed me, peeling off layers of muddy clothing as she went. 'It was good,' she said to me, as if I'd shown any interest whatsoever. 'But I still don't see why we couldn't have shirts and protein drinks and everything that the boys are getting. We deserve them.'

'Yeah, well, people don't always get what they deserve,' I said. 'You might think you deserve special shirts and drinks, or a best friend who doesn't lie to you, but that doesn't mean that that's what you're going to get.'

'It's not very fair,' Chloe said, pushing open the bathroom door.

'No,' I said. 'It's not.'

Then I did something a bit stupid. You'd think by now that I'd know that I'm not very good at having a sensible conversation with anyone when I'm angry, but I wanted some answers. So I phoned Lauren.

Except Lauren didn't answer. Her mum did.

'She's resting, Amelia,' she said. She sounded annoyed before I'd even said a word. But I was annoyed too.

'I need to speak to her,' I said. If she wasn't going to bother to be polite, neither was I.

'I'll see if she feels up to calling you later,' she said as if she was doing me a huge favour.

'This is really important.'

She sighed. 'I'm sure you think it's important, Amelia. But, if you don't mind me saying, you sound rather aggressive and I can only assume that once again there's some sort of issue between you and Lauren, which, as I believe I've mentioned, disrupts the peace and calm that Lauren needs at the moment.'

'It's not me that's being disruptive!' I said.

'Please don't shout. I know that Lauren wasn't entirely clear about her condition before but you do understand now that she has a serious illness, don't you? She really needs you to be considerate.'

The image of Lauren and Josh flashed into my mind again. 'She's the one being inconsiderate!' I snapped.

'Amelia,' she said in a voice of ice. 'This selfish behaviour is not helping Lauren. I trust you won't continue this silliness when you see her at school.'

And she rang off.

Unbelievable. What a witch! I was so angry I was shaking. She was treating me like a selfish toddler, as if Lauren was a perfect angel who I was making sick. The way she'd said 'serious illness' made it sound as if Lauren was gasping her last breath and I was just bothering her with my silly complaints about the fact she'd lied to me again. My chest felt like someone was piling bricks on top of me. I could hardly catch my breath. I lay on my bed and the tears started to fall. And they kept on coming.

CHAPTER ✦ TWENTY-FIVE

I don't think anyone noticed my blotchy face at teatime. Once I'd stopped bawling, I decided that I didn't want to talk to anyone about Lauren. I'd already snapped at Chloe earlier and I didn't want to bring anyone else down by talking about my rubbish life.

Instead, I agreed to play cards with Ella and Chloe. There's no TV at Dad's house because Suvi says it rots the imagination so Ella and Chloe are always playing cards, as if it was during the war or something. I usually say no, but this time I was glad to have something to concentrate on.

'What did you eat at the cinema?' Chloe asked Ella, while she dealt out the cards.

When you go to see a film, normal people ask you what you thought of it, but Chloe doesn't care about that; she just likes to hear what snacks you ate while you were watching it.

'I had one of those little tubs of ice cream,' Ella said.

'What flavour?'

'Chocolate.'

'You should've got some of those nachos. I love that runny cheese they put on them.'

'We've all seen you eating nachos with runny cheese,' I said. 'And I'm pretty sure no one wants to be reminded of that image.' I turned to Ella. 'Was the film good?'

'It was OK.' Her forehead was creased again.

'Was Crystal all right today?' I asked.

Ella studied her cards carefully.

Chloe nudged Ella. 'What did she do?'

'She never does anything bad to me,' Ella insisted.

I laid down a card. 'So who was she bad to?'

'She was rude to the lady selling the tickets. And after the film was over and we were leaving she said, "I'm not coming back to this dump again." It was really embarrassing.'

'She sounds horrible,' Chloe said.

Ella sighed. 'But she's not horrible other times. She's never mean to people at school, not like Jasmine is.'

Jasmine is the meanest girl in Ella's class. She's

so mean that she's even horrible to Ella and that's like being nasty to a kitten.

Ella screwed up her face. 'Ashandra says that Crystal talks about herself a lot, but I don't really mind that because she does lots of interesting things and she's fun and she's generous.'

Chloe looked surprised. 'Do you mean you like her because she gives you stuff?'

'Of course she doesn't,' I said. That didn't sound like Ella at all.

'She *does* give people chocolate and presents and things,' Ella said thoughtfully. 'But she does other things too, like she spent ages helping me and Kayleigh at hockey. I don't understand how anyone who's kind like that can be so horrible to their mum and nice cinema ladies that smile at you.'

'People aren't just all good or all bad,' I pointed out. 'Look at me: you'd think that someone as obviously brilliant and intelligent as me would never have blazing rows with people but I have been known to.'

Ella chewed her lip.

'I don't think you have to tie yourself in knots trying to understand Crystal,' I said. 'The way she talks to people makes you uncomfortable so I don't think you should hang around with her.'

Ella's eyes widened. 'I can't stop being friends with her because of this. She'd think it was silly.'

'But *you* don't think it's silly. You get to choose your friends.'

Ella's face cleared. 'Really?'

'Really,' I said.

'Except us two,' Chloe said, pointing a finger at herself and then me. 'You're stuck with us two.'

After a while, Chloe wanted to play Slam and since only two can play that game I left them to it. I drifted out into the hallway. Dad leant out of his study. 'Everything all right?' he asked.

I shrugged non-committally.

'Come in,' he said and he pulled the other chair up next to his. 'How's Lauren?' he asked, turning away from his computer to face me. He's definitely much better at giving people his full attention these days.

I wasn't sure it was a good idea for me to start talking about Lauren; my anger had mostly faded away, but I was still confused and upset.

'She's OK,' I said. Then I couldn't help adding, 'I don't really understand what's going on with her; it's like sometimes she's too sick to do anything and then other times she seems completely fine.'

'I think that's how it is with CFS,' Dad said.

I heard Lauren's mum's voice in my head asking if I understood that Lauren had a serious illness and an uncomfortable feeling started bubbling up in my stomach as I realised that I knew very little at all about CFS.

'Are you feeling OK?' Dad asked. 'You seem a bit out of sorts.'

'I'm just, you know . . . thinking about things.'

'Anything in particular?'

I shook my head.

He opened his drawer and offered me a piece of fudge from his secret stash. We chewed for a minute.

'What would you like to do tomorrow?' Dad asked. 'I haven't seen much of you this weekend.'

'Will the library be open?' I asked.

'Not on Sundays. Is it for homework?'

'No, I thought maybe I could find out a bit more about CFS; Suvi says that books can help you learn about anything you can think of.'

Dad struggled so hard not to show his surprise that I was quoting Suvi that I almost laughed.

'I think I ought to learn some more about it.' I rubbed my eyebrow. 'I should've done it before. I was a bit stupid and I just sort of assumed that the doctors would make it go away.'

'It's tough when you realise that's not always possible.' He patted my knee. 'You know another great source of information on any topic you can think of?'

I shrugged.

'People. And not just people who write books. There must be a lot of people who have experienced what Lauren's going through and thanks to modern technology . . .' he pointed to his laptop, 'you can hear what some of them have got to say.' He tapped away for a moment and then swung his laptop round so I could see what he'd found. It was a forum for CFS sufferers.

I don't know why I didn't think of that before. 'Thanks!'

Dad pushed back his chair. 'Take as long as you like. I'm going to make a phone call.' He picked up his mobile and left the room.

I pulled my chair close to the desk. I don't know why but I'd sort of assumed that Dad would hang around and talk a bit more. Maybe he hadn't changed quite as much as I'd thought.

I scanned down the page of thread titles and clicked on *Is it just me that finds other people's reactions to CFS hard to handle?* The first post was by a woman who said she'd been suffering from CFS for years and that one of the most difficult things about it was that many of her so-called friends didn't seem to believe that it was a real illness. Other posters replied saying how people had told them that they were lazy or that they didn't 'look ill'. I squirmed when I read that one. I knew I'd said that to Lauren a few times.

I spent an hour reading different threads. Every time I thought I'd found the saddest story, I came across another one. There was a woman who hadn't been able to travel to her son's wedding. There was a man whose girlfriend had left him because she thought his illness was all in his head. And, over and over again, people spoke about feeling betrayed by their body and simply not having the energy to even get dressed in the morning. When dad came back to his study, I was crying.

'Amelia!' He wrapped me up in a big hug. 'What is it, sweetheart?'

'It's so horrible,' I gulped. 'Poor Lauren.' I wasn't making much sense but Dad took a look at the computer screen and I think he got the general gist.

He squeezed me tight and said, 'It's all right,' until I got my sobs under control.

'Listen,' he said, wiping my tears with a tissue. 'You mustn't scare yourself with stories from the internet.'

'But they're true,' I sniffed. 'All these poor people have got CFS and it's terrible.' The tears started falling again.

'I know,' he said soothingly. 'It's rotten that this is happening to Lauren.' He smoothed my soggy hair away from my face. 'What you have to remember is that the people who are posting here are probably at their lowest ebb. The internet is a useful tool, but you've got to keep in mind that it does have its limitations.'

'What do you mean?'

'Who do you think is most likely to write a post on this forum? A CFS sufferer who's having a bad patch so they're stuck in bed, maybe with no one to talk to, or a CFS sufferer who's doing well and is out having a good time with their friends?'

I supposed he had a point there. 'But the bad patches do happen.'

'Of course, and I don't think it hurts for you to know how tough things can be for someone with CFS, but it won't help you or Lauren to dwell on it.'

I suddenly felt tired. When my dad had come into the room and wrapped me up in his jumpery hug, I'd thought that everything was going to be all right; that he'd fix things like he did when I was a little kid. But he couldn't fix it any more than the doctors could fix Lauren.

'I've just been speaking to my friend, Azra,' Dad said. 'Remember we went to her barbeque last summer? She's the doctor.'

'I remember.'

'I asked her what she knew about CFS.'

So he hadn't disappeared to make a work call. My tears nearly started again. He wasn't leaving me to it; he'd been doing his own research for me. I swallowed. 'What did she say?'

'Well . . . it's a difficult condition. Not everyone is in agreement about what exactly it is or the best way to treat it.'

'Does Azra have patients with CFS?'

'She's not allowed to talk to me about individual cases because their details are confidential. But she did tell me that in the course of her career she's seen a wide-ranging level of impact of the condition.'

'What does that mean?'

'It means that sometimes people are confined to their beds for long periods of time, while some have cycles of improvement followed by relapse, but then others learn to manage their condition in a way that means that they can live something approaching a normal life. She'd even heard of sufferers who completely recover.'

'Really?'

'Yep.'

I took a long breath. 'So Lauren might get better,' I said. 'Or she might get better and then relapse.' I thought about the first stories I'd read. 'Or it might just be awful for her the whole time.'

Dad looked serious. 'You have to hope for the best,' he said.

'But what if she never gets better?'

'Then I'm certain that you'll be there to help her through it. You can't influence Lauren's health so it's no use worrying about it. Concentrate on what you can do and that's being a good friend.'

He was right. I knew that I wouldn't be looking up any more sad stories. I was glad that I had a clearer picture of what CFS meant because now I could appreciate what Lauren was going through, but getting depressed about it wasn't helpful.

Dad pulled me in for another hug. 'I know it's hard,' he said. 'But I'm here if you need to talk about it.'

And I felt better because, even though I was growing up and I knew that some of the problems I'd come across now wouldn't be the kind that my dad could fix with glue or words or ice cream, I also realised that he'd always be there beside me, whatever I was going through. And so would my mum. And even Suvi. Some difficult things can't be made better but they're easier to get through if you have someone special by your side. I hoped I could be one of those people for Lauren.

CHAPTER ❤ TWENTY-SIX

I went to bed early, but I couldn't sleep. At midnight, I was still thinking about Lauren and the things her mum had said to me on the phone. Had I really been selfish? I turned my pillow over to the cool side and tried to relax, but Kirsti was stirring in the next room and a few seconds later she started to whimper loudly. I thought maybe I could shush her back to sleep before she woke Suvi up so I slipped into her room and scooped her out of her cot.

'*Shh*, baby,' I whispered, patting her softly on the back like I'd seen Suvi do. Kirsti was warm and soft and it was actually really nice giving her a cuddle. I rocked her gently and she closed her eyes. In a few minutes, I was pretty sure she was asleep again. I didn't want to jolt her awake so, very slowly, I leant over the cot and lowered her back down. Once I'd managed it, I stood watching her for a while. Babies are a bit noisy and dribbly, but they do look quite sweet when they're asleep.

I tiptoed out of her room and walked straight into someone.

I gasped, but it was only Suvi in her dressing gown.

'Is she . . .?' she asked.

'She's gone back to sleep.'

Suvi's shoulders sagged. 'Did she wake you?'

'I wasn't asleep.'

'Why is that? Are you OK, Amelia?'

'I'm fine.'

The only light was coming from the bathroom, but even in the shadow I could see dark circles under Suvi's eyes. 'You should get back to sleep,' I said.

Suvi tucked her hair behind her ears. 'I don't think I can,' she said. 'Every time I'm almost going to sleep, I think that I hear Kirsti crying.'

'You look terrible,' I said.

'I do,' she agreed.

I remembered how Ella knew exactly how to take care of Suvi when she was looking shattered the other day. 'I could make you a cup of tea,' I said.

Suvi seemed a bit surprised by this, which I

suppose is understandable. I don't think I'd ever made her a cup of tea before.

'OK,' she said. 'Maybe some camomile tea will help me to sleep.'

So we crept downstairs and I put the kettle on.

Suvi pulled her dressing gown more tightly round herself and sank into a chair. I tried to think of something helpful to say, but I couldn't come up with anything so I got the milk out of the fridge instead.

'Thank you, Amelia,' Suvi said. 'It was kind of you to look after Kirsti.'

'That's OK. It didn't take long for her to go back to sleep.'

Suvi made a snorting noise. 'For me, it takes ages every time to get her to sleep. Maybe you should show me what it is that you do.'

'Actually, I just did what I've seen you doing.'

'Oh.' She seemed strangely pleased by that.

I made the tea. Camomile for Suvi, which smells like hand cream, and normal for me.

'Can you tell me why it is that you're not sleeping?' Suvi asked.

I switched my mug from my right to my left hand. 'I was just thinking. About the concert and Christmas and everything.'

Suvi narrowed her eyes. 'Amelia, I think that

you're trying too hard not to be the girl who complains any more.'

I shifted uncomfortably in my seat. Obviously, I have been trying to be less negative, but I didn't think that anyone had noticed. I wasn't sure that I wanted anyone to notice.

'I think it's good not to say every little thing that you don't like, otherwise it's very boring to listen to.'

Was she saying that I used to be annoying to listen to?

'But you don't have to keep away everything you're thinking. Sometimes things are hard and it's good to talk about them.'

'Hmm.' Maybe she was right. I used to want to make everybody miserable when I was miserable, but recently I've done the complete opposite and not spoken to anyone about Lauren. Even when I'd been talking to Dad about CFS earlier, I hadn't told him anything about what happened today with Lauren's mum. 'I don't want to bring other people down.'

'There's a difference between spreading your bad feelings about and telling someone your problems.'

I sighed. 'I'm having some problems with Lauren. I feel like she never shares things with me any more. Important things.'

185

'I see. Have you spoken to Lauren about this?'

'Not really. It's hard to find a good time.'

'Why don't you go to her house tomorrow?'

'I don't think her mum will let me in.'

Suvi blinked in surprise. 'Why not?'

'She doesn't like me.'

Suvi tutted. 'Why would she not like a girl like you?'

Which surprised me because I've been pretty horrible to Suvi in the past so I'd have thought she could think of lots of reasons why people wouldn't like me.

'You're a great girl,' Suvi said. 'You're smart and funny and loyal.'

I couldn't help snorting then. 'Lauren's mum doesn't know anything about that; she thinks I make Lauren's illness worse.'

'And do you?'

'No! I didn't really understand about CFS before because she didn't tell me. She was always saying she was fine or pretending she was off school for something different. And then, when I did find out, it took me a while to really understand what it means. In fact, I think I'm still working it out, but I want to help Lauren, I really do.'

'Does her mother know this?'

'No. But it doesn't matter anyway.' I looked at Suvi. I didn't get why she was making a thing of this. She never cares what people think of her. She's not at all afraid of saying stuff that might make others not like her. 'You're not normally bothered by what people think,' I said.

'If people know all about you and they say, "I don't like this," that's fine. But this woman doesn't know about you. She misunderstands. She sees a cross girl who likes to scowl and say rude things, but she doesn't see the good Amelia.'

I didn't know I had a good side. 'What good Amelia?'

Suvi took a sip of tea. 'Some people are naturally very sweet and caring and giving . . .'

'That's not me,' I said.

Suvi smiled. 'No, that is not you. But some people, even though they have a lot of angry, sad feelings, try to be a good person for their friends and family. Helping others is not the easiest thing for you but you try very hard to do it.'

'Do I?'

'You cook for your tired mother. You try to stop the worries of little Ella. You even hold the baby for your wicked stepmother.'

I didn't know Suvi had noticed any of that stuff.

'And I think Lauren's mother needs to know that

you try to be a good friend to Lauren. Then she can decide if she likes you.'

'But how can she know what sort of friend I am?'

'You have to tell her.'

I couldn't see that happening. She wouldn't let me get a word in edgeways for a start.

Suvi topped up my tea from the pot. 'I'm glad you told me this and I know your father is happy that you two talked today; you don't have to have problems all alone.'

'Neither do you,' I said.

'What do you mean?'

I was very close to telling her outright that I could see she wasn't managing with Kirsti but I thought that might upset her, so instead I said, 'I think you're tired. Kirsti is . . . being difficult and maybe you could do with some help.'

Suvi seemed amused. 'I think you're changing this talk from you to me.'

'You've already given me some good advice. I think you need some help.'

Suvi tucked her hair behind her ears. 'Your father does help. He's very good at settling Kirsti, but he has to get some sleep so he can go to work in the morning. He cannot go to Kirsti each time she cries. Sometimes it must be me.'

'Can't he tell you what it is that he does to get her to sleep?'

Suvi pulled a face. 'He's good at the doing, but not so good at the explaining.'

'I know who could help you. Someone who knows a lot about babies.'

'Who's that?'

'My mum.'

Suvi nodded. 'That's true. All you girls were babies once.'

'And she must have taught us how to sleep because we all do it now. Even Lucy. Although she does like to make traps in her bed, so when you're doing something perfectly innocent – like trying to steal her hot-water bottle – you have to watch out in case she's left something spiky or a bit of old sandwich in there. Actually, I'm not sure that the sandwich is part of the trap. I think she just likes to have snacks in her bed.'

'Yes, she does.' Suvi seemed to agree with this so strongly that I suspected that she might have found the remains of snacks in Lucy's bed here.

'Anyway, if you want help with babies, you should speak to my mum.' I promise I was trying to be helpful with that suggestion. And maybe there was a tiny bit of me that wanted to see if Suvi could take her own advice. Mum and Dad and Suvi all act like they're very mature about the divorce and that they can still get along, but I wondered if Suvi would actually want to listen to Mum telling her what to do.

Suvi was thinking. 'Yes,' she said. 'You're completely right. Your mother is the best expert on children that I know. I'll telephone her tomorrow.' She took her mug to the sink and rinsed it out. 'Now we must go to bed and have some sleep before Kirsti wakes up again.'

We tiptoed upstairs and just as I was going into my room Suvi reached out and gave my shoulder a gentle squeeze.

The last time Suvi tried to squeeze me was in the summer when I bent down in the kitchen to get some plates and I stood up and gashed my head on the corner of the cupboard door above that someone had left open. I had to have six stitches. While we were at the hospital waiting for Mum and Dad to arrive, I might have been crying a tiny bit and Suvi tried to put her arm round me and I shouted, 'Don't touch me!'

But I didn't mind at all this time.

CHAPTER ✦ TWENTY–SEVEN

I'll say one thing about Suvi: she doesn't hang around. By the time I'd dragged myself out of bed on Sunday morning, she'd already had a long conversation with my mum.

'She was very helpful,' Suvi said. 'She gave me lots of ideas. For now, I'm taking Kirsti in the car to help her have her nap. Will you come with me?'

'Er . . .' Hanging out with Suvi wasn't top of my list of things to do on a Sunday but I supposed I didn't have a lot else to do. 'OK.'

I polished off my toast, cleaned my teeth and got into the car. Kirsti was grizzling and I really hoped she wasn't going to do that the entire time. But Mum obviously knew what she was talking about because, as soon as the car started, Kirsti settled down and in minutes she was asleep.

Suvi was chatting away about getting a Christmas tree when I realised which road we were on. It was the one leading to Lauren's. Then Suvi turned off and there we were: parked outside Lauren's house.

'What are we doing here?' I asked.

'We agreed that you would talk to Lauren's mother, yes?'

Actually, I distinctly remembered being careful not to specifically agree to Suvi's plan. 'I don't know . . .' I said.

'You're unhappy. You need to take action.'

I supposed that was true. 'Did you tell Lauren's mum I was coming?' I asked.

'No. This is for you to do.'

My heart sank. It obviously showed on my face because Suvi said, 'I know it's hard. There are many words I could say to this woman, but it's important that you learn to do these things for yourself. You girls, you're like little birds; when you're tiny like Kirsti and Lucy, then we can do everything for you, then, when you're bigger, we take you to the edge of the branch . . .' She gestured out of the window at Lauren's house. 'And we push you off.'

I pulled a face. 'What happens then?'

'Then,' she smiled, 'you fly! All by yourself.'

Even though I wasn't really into this whole

comparing me to a bird thing, I understood what she was saying. I had to sort out this problem for myself.

I opened the car door.

'Do you want me to wait for you?' Suvi asked.

'That's OK,' I said. 'I can walk back. And Suvi?'

'Yes?'

'Thanks.'

Suvi looked back at Kirsti's sleeping face.

'Thank you too.'

Then I got out of the car and walked up to door and I couldn't help wondering about all those baby birds being taught to fly by their parents. The idea of striking out from the tree and soaring into the sky was all very nice, but what if I just landed with a splat on the pavement below?

Lauren's mum looked slightly less annoyed than the last time I saw her, which I hoped was a good sign. She opened her mouth and I knew she was going to tell me that Lauren was asleep or resting or busy with a secret date.

'Hello, Mrs Anderson. I wondered if I could talk to you,' I said, before she could get a word out.

'Oh.'

That surprised her.

'You'd better come in.'

She took me into the sitting room. The house

seemed very still. I guessed that either Lauren was out or she was asleep.

'Sit down.'

I perched on the edge of the sofa. 'I wanted to say . . .' I stopped. I wasn't entirely sure what it was that I did want to say. 'I've never meant to upset Lauren,' I said. 'I didn't completely understand about how sick she was before. Even after she told me she was ill, she didn't tell me that much about her illness. She doesn't really like talking about it.'

I saw some recognition in her eyes. 'Lauren is rather keen to downplay her symptoms.'

'But now I've found out a bit more about CFS and I know that she gets tired easily and I promise you I'm keeping an eye on her.'

Lauren's mum was still giving me her full attention without interrupting so I decided to press on.

'And it might seem like we fall out all the time, but we honestly don't. And, even when there is a bit of . . . drama, it always gets sorted out.' As I was saying this, I realised how much I meant it. I knew that whatever was going on with Josh, I wasn't going to fall out with Lauren over it. 'I never stop wanting to be friends with Lauren. She's my best friend.'

There was a pause. Lauren's mum drew a hand across her face.

'I think I owe you an apology, Amelia,' she said

slowly. 'It's been a difficult six months. When your child is ill, it's always distressing, but this has been particularly hard because, until recently, we had no idea what was wrong. I've tried to protect Lauren, and with Lauren's father away so much I felt like I had to be very firm in that respect, but I realise now that I've been rather harsh. You see, for a while I thought it was in her best interests for her to see much less of her friends. I deliberately tried to discourage you from visiting and I'm sorry for that, Amelia.'

I could hardly believe that she was admitting her mistake.

'I honestly thought I was doing the best thing for Lauren, but I appreciate now that she needs friends just as much as she needs her rest. She's far happier on the days when she sees you.'

I was really glad to hear that.

'I was so desperate not to tire Lauren out that I resented anyone who required any of her energy. I'm sorry that I've been rude to you; all your visits and phone calls and cards ought to have led me to see what a loyal friend you are.' She'd been staring at the carpet all this time, but now she lifted her eyes to me. 'Lauren needs you very much and I do hope that I haven't put you off coming round.'

Incredible. I don't know exactly what I was expecting when I stepped through the door, but it definitely wasn't this. 'No,' I said. 'It hasn't put me off at all.'

'But you do understand that sometimes she just might not be up to seeing you? And it's no reflection on how she feels about you as a friend.'

I hadn't really got that before. I'd thought that because Lauren had a diagnosis it meant she was going to get better quickly. But after everything I'd learnt yesterday I could see much more clearly that Lauren's illness wasn't going to just disappear. 'I understand that now.'

'Mum!' Lauren called from upstairs.

'Sounds like she's awake. Would you like to go up and see her?'

I could tell that she had to choke back adding on something like 'just for a little while' so I said, 'I promise I won't stay long.'

Lauren was surprised to see me coming up the stairs. 'I didn't know you were coming round,' she said.

'Just thought I'd pop in and see you,' I said.

We went into her bedroom and sat down, but I felt awkward. It was all very well deciding that I wasn't going to fall out with Lauren about her seeing Josh, but it felt like there was a secret sitting between us on the bed like a big hairy monster. At least it did to me. Lauren was beaming.

'Guess what?' she said in a low voice.

'What?'

'Yesterday I managed to persuade Mum that I was feeling OK enough to go to the post office on my own and who do you think I bumped into?'

Oh. *Ohhhhhhhhh.* 'Josh,' I said. And I knew I was right.

'Yes! I mean, literally I walked round the corner and he almost knocked me over on his bike and then he said sorry, and I said that's all right and then we ended up sitting outside KFC! Can you believe it?'

I felt like a terrible person. I don't know why I'd assumed that Lauren was keeping all this a big secret. Maybe it was something to do with her not being entirely honest about her illness, but I was really, really glad that I hadn't launched into an attack on her and that I'd had the chance to see that she had clearly been dying to tell me her news.

'Then what happened?' I asked.

'He asked why I wasn't in maths.'

'Whoooo!' I said. 'He's obviously missed you.'

She blushed. 'We actually had a really nice talk ... and he asked me to go to Olivia's New Year's Eve party with him.'

My stomach clenched.

'But I didn't say yes.'

'Why not?'

'Because I know you like him too and you're way more important to me.'

It was so sweet that she'd said that, but, even though I felt kind of jealous, I knew that I couldn't let her give up a date with Josh just for me. 'You have to say yes,' I said. 'I honestly don't mind.' Even though I did a tiny bit.

'Are you sure?'

I nodded hard. Surprisingly, I didn't feel quite as bad as I might have expected. Josh was cute and he seemed nice, but I'd never even really spoken to him. 'I always knew he liked you. What exactly did you say to him? It isn't too late for you to accept his invitation, is it?'

'I sort of didn't say anything. He told me to think about it, so I guess I can still say yes.' She couldn't keep the excitement out of her voice. 'If you're completely sure that it's OK with you.'

'It is.' Then something made me say, 'Anyway, I think I might be interested in someone else.'

'No way! Who?'

And I realised that maybe there was someone. Someone with big dark eyes, who was always making me laugh and who liked singing as much as I did.

So then we spent the next half-hour discussing whether Bartek would say yes if I asked him to the party.

CHAPTER ❤ TWENTY-EIGHT

Finally, things at school were how I'd been wanting them to be all term. Or at least they were close enough. Lauren still had to go home at lunchtime and she couldn't do PE, but we were chatting and sharing secrets again and it no longer felt like there was some sort of invisible barrier between us.

Walking to Dad's on Wednesday, we were all really cheerful. Chloe was delighted because rugby was going so well and the other girls at training kept telling her how great she was for getting in the paper and making the Chiefs start the girls' squad. Ella seemed like a weight had been lifted from her shoulders. 'How are things with Crystal?' I asked.

'Fine,' she said. 'I've just been hanging out with Ashandra and Kayleigh and sort of keeping my distance from Crystal. She's got loads of other friends to talk to anyway.'

I smiled at her. I felt quite smiley towards everyone these days. I even felt more friendly towards Suvi. She was quite human and actually a little bit nice after all. When we got to Dad's house, I said, 'Hi, Suvi!' so enthusiastically that Chloe and Ella stared at me.

'Hi to you all!' she said back.

'How's Kirsti?' I asked. 'Is she sleeping well?'

Suvi gave a rueful smile. 'Maybe just a little better. We're trying A Routine.'

I wasn't entirely sure what A Routine involved, but it seemed to have given Suvi hope.

'That's great,' I said and I strolled into the kitchen. Lucy was there, under the table again, eating cereal and flicking through the pages of her friends book. I was feeling so upbeat that, instead of pointing out that she had both a milk moustache and a milk beard, I said, 'All right, shortie?'

'Urgh,' she spat and picked up a felt tip to scribble something out.

'What's the matter?' I asked.

'Nothing.'

She scribbled something else.

'What are you doing?'

'Mum said I can take two people to the play centre on Sunday.'

'Who are you going to take?'

'I'm counting their points.'

I poured myself a glass of juice. 'I see, so you're finally going to reward the top scorers, huh? Who are the lucky winners?' Personally, I was routing for Evil Emily; at least she'd attempted to stand up to Lucy.

Lucy gave the sort of sigh that grown-ups do when they have to fill in a very long form. 'I'm still counting.'

'Let's have a look.' I took the book out of her hands and flipped through the pages. It was pretty hard to understand. 'How come you've changed this bit? Mia had two points here for giving you her crisps and you've crossed them out.'

'They were cheese and onion.'

'And what about here? She got a point for sharing her pens with you and that's crossed out too.'

'Her green doesn't work.'

I skimmed through the rest of it. It looked like Mia had been a clear winner, but Lucy had gone back through her book and knocked off lots of her points for silly reasons.

I crouched down beside her. 'Do you know what I think? I think you already know who you want to take to the play centre. It's Rose and Emily, isn't it?'

'But they haven't got the highest scores.'

'Does it matter?'

'But that's how it works. The people with the most points are the best friends.'

I felt quite old and wise. 'But are they?'

Lucy scowled. 'I can't just choose who I like! That's not how the book works.'

'It's your book. You can do what you like with it.'

I watched her face smooth out as she took that in. 'I can, can't I?'

I nodded, then I took my juice into the sitting room and as I sat down on the sofa I heard the lid of the bin clang shut.

CHAPTER TWENTY-NINE

The next day, I was eating lunch with Lauren when Ella came rushing up to me.

'What's the matter?' I asked.

'It's Crystal. She asked me to go to her house.'

Poor Ella; she was clearly all stressed out again. 'What did you say?'

'I said I had to ask Mum, but she thought that was a yes.'

'Why didn't you just say no?'

Ella's face crumpled. 'I thought she'd ask me why and I didn't know what I'd say.'

'It's all right; you can tell her that you're busy.'

'But she might ask me again another time.'

'And you can say you're busy that time too. She'll get the message eventually.'

Ella twisted her hands. 'That doesn't seem very honest.'

'It's either that or tell her the truth.'

The colour drained from her face. 'I suppose I could tell her I'm busy.'

I looked at my watch. Lunchtime was nearly over. 'Listen, you're walking home with me after your tutor captains' meeting, aren't you? We can talk about it then.'

She went off to her lesson, but it was clear she was going to worry all afternoon.

Rehearsal was fun. Whenever Mr Garcia got on a rant, Bartek waggled his eyebrows at me.

When Mr Garcia turned his attention to another soloist, Bartek leant over and said, 'Today, in English, you were very good in the debate.'

'Thanks. And thanks for voting for my team.'

'You were the best. Some of the people were so quiet and they have nothing to say. You were very . . . powerful.'

I laughed. 'So you're saying I'm good at shouting? I've got four little sisters; I get a lot of practice.'

'Really? I have three brothers! There is a lot of shouting at my house too. And when it's time to eat it's like this . . .' He mimed rapidly stuffing his face, while keeping a protective arm round his plate.

He looked like Chloe does when it's pizza for tea.

I nodded. 'If you can't eat it fast, you don't get to eat it.'

Then we had to do some more singing, but I thought next rehearsal I might ask Bartek about his brothers. And maybe work my way round to Olivia's party.

When Mr Garcia dismissed us, Ella was waiting for me outside the hall. Her face was flushed.

'Crystal was at the meeting!' she said. 'Her class tutor captain is off sick so she came instead.'

'Did you tell her you can't come to her house?'

'I was going to, but I didn't. I hardly said anything to her and now she thinks I'm being weird.'

I could only imagine that Ella's behaviour probably did seem pretty weird.

Ella grabbed my arm. She was staring hard at a girl at the other end of the corridor.

'Is that her?' I asked.

'Yes.'

'Why don't you speak to her now?'

Ella was still clutching my elbow. 'I can't.'

'OK. You don't have to.'

'But I should.' She nodded her head decisively. 'I'm going to do it.'

I squeezed her hand. Ella is pretty cool and she's much braver than she thinks she is. If I was as afraid of things as Ella is, I don't think I'd leave the house.

'Hey, Crystal!' Ella called and she rushed up the corridor to speak to her. I followed more slowly.

'Hi, Ella,' Crystal said. She sounded friendly enough, but I decided to hang back by the noticeboard and listen to how things went.

'Can I talk to you about something?' Ella asked.

'What is it?' Crystal asked.

'I . . .' Ella faltered. 'I don't think I want to come to your house any more.'

There was a pause. 'What's wrong with my house?'

'Nothing! It's just . . . I feel uncomfortable about the way you speak to your mum.'

'What are you talking about? What about my mum?'

I tensed. If Crystal was going to get nasty then I was definitely going to interrupt.

'I don't think you're very . . . kind to her,' Ella said quietly.

Crystal sucked in her breath. 'That's rubbish. I'm not horrible to my mum. Anyway, who do you think you are? How I speak to her is none of your business.'

'I know.'

'I can do what I like.'

'I know.'

'Maybe I don't like the way *you* talk. You can't stop me thinking what I think.'

'That's true, but *I* think it's really important to be nice. And I know that's not important to some people, but it is to me, so I'm just saying that I don't think I want to be friends with someone who's rude to people.'

'It was fine when you were laughing at everyone I was saying funny things about.'

'I never laughed at that; I don't think hurt feelings are funny.'

I was sure that was true and Crystal must have known it too because she said, 'Yeah, well, plenty of my friends think it is funny, so I don't need to hang out with a boring geek like you.'

Ella didn't reply.

'What's the matter?' Crystal sneered. 'Bet you've got some rude things to say about me now.'

'I don't want to start a fight.' Ella's voice trembled. 'I really liked playing hockey with you. I think you're fun and you're really nice when you like people. I just don't feel comfortable when you're rude.'

'But I'm not rude to you! Or any of my mates. I'm not rude to anyone who matters.'

'I think everyone matters.'

'Then you're dumb!' Crystal snapped and she walked off.

I rushed over to Ella. 'Are you OK?'

Her face was white and her eyes were watery. She nodded, but she couldn't speak. I put my arm round her and she took some deep breaths.

'She said I'm dumb,' Ella said. 'Do you think she's right? Do you think it's stupid to fall out with someone because of how they talk to the lady in the cinema?'

'No, you're absolutely right to care about the way people treat each other. I'm certain that you're definitely right.' I looked at Crystal slamming through the double doors. 'And you know what? I think Crystal knows it too.'

CHAPTER ✿ THIRTY

On Saturday afternoon, Mum took us Christmas shopping. Lucy had been going on about it forever.

'I don't know why you're so bothered,' I said, once we were all crammed into the car. 'You don't normally give much thought to our presents; last year, you gave me one of Chloe's T-shirts. I wouldn't have minded, but you'd got it out of the washing basket and it had ketchup all down it.'

'I'm not doing shopping for humans today,' Lucy said with more scorn than I think a seven-year-old ought to be using.

'What do you mean, not shopping for humans?' Chloe asked. 'Who are you shopping for then? Aliens?'

'I am shopping for my animals,' Lucy said.

Chloe pulled a face. 'Well, I'm not buying you a present until you buy me one.'

'I'm not sure that's really in the spirit of Christmas,' Mum said.

'I've got enough Christmas spirit to pretend to like it when Lucy gives me a washing-up brush, but I haven't got enough to be happy when she takes my good present and gives me nothing at all in return.'

Then there was a bit of a row while Chloe and Lucy debated whether various gifts they've given each other, including a tin of cat-shaped spaghetti, a selection of pebbles and a home-made jelly mould, were worth anything at all.

When we actually got to the shops, I was already quite tired.

We worked our way up the high street and by the time we reached the clock tower we were all carrying several bags. Mum said she needed a break so we were heading up in the lift to the café in the department store when the doors opened and Mum's 'friend' Greg got in.

'Louise!' he said to Mum. 'Fancy seeing you here.' He tore his eyes off her to notice the rest of us were there and said, 'Hello, girls!' His eyes widened as if he couldn't quite believe how many of us there were. Although he must have known how many kids Mum's got because obviously she must talk about us all the time. Maybe he couldn't quite believe how much space we were taking up. That's because Lucy had insisted on bringing her entire hedgehog family in a huge old hiking rucksack of Dad's. That, plus all our shopping and Chloe's ginormous behind, pretty much filled the lift.

'How are you, Amelia?' he asked. He seemed pleased with himself that he'd remembered my name.

'I'm shopping with my little sisters,' I said. 'So obviously I'm in heaven. Any second now I'm going to break into an uplifting musical dance number.'

He snorted. It's nice to finally meet someone who appreciates sarcasm.

'You won't think it's funny when she actually does start singing,' Lucy said.

'You must be Lucy,' Greg said.

'Of course,' Lucy said. 'What would you buy a hedgehog for Christmas?'

'Er . . .'

'I'm Chloe,' Chloe said, elbowing Lucy out of the way. 'I'm getting an England shirt for Christmas. Did you know that I helped to persuade the Chiefs to set up a girls' youth squad?'

'I did not know that. Congratulations.'

'Thank you. If there's something you think is really sexist, you can write to the newspaper about it if you like.'

'Oh.' His eyes slide sideways to Mum. 'Well, I'll certainly consider that.' He turned to Ella. 'Have you bought anything nice?'

Ella nodded and turned bright pink.

There was a long pause while everyone waited for Ella to tell him what she'd bought, but she didn't, so eventually Mum said, 'Which floor did you want?'

'Ah, the third. I'm looking for gloves for my sister.'

So Mum pressed the button and up we went again.

'Gloves wouldn't be very good for hedgehogs,' Lucy said scornfully as if Greg had suggested them.

'No,' he agreed. 'A scarf might be better for a hedgehog.'

The lift stopped and the doors opened. Greg smiled at Mum. 'Best get on then.'

'Yes, nice to see you.'

'I hope you find your hedgehog scarf,' he said to Lucy. 'And good luck with the rugby ...' He hesitated. I think he'd forgotten Chloe's name.

'Thanks,' Chloe said.

'Sorry to miss that musical number, Amelia.'

I grinned. I couldn't help being pleased that I was the one whose name he got right.

He stepped out of the lift and turned back to look at Ella. 'Enjoy your shopping.'

Ella said nothing.

'Ella,' hissed Chloe.

But still Ella didn't say anything.

'Right,' Greg said. 'I'll, er, OK, so . . . bye again.' And he backed away, giving a little wave, until he bumped into a mannequin dressed in a fluffy coat.

Lucy cackled with laughter.

'Lucy!' Mum said in a low voice.

'I'm just laughing. You can't keep laughs in. Or farts. If you do, you explode.'

'*Shhhh*,' I said. Seriously. My sisters are so embarrassing. Fortunately, at that point, the doors finally slid shut.

'At least I say things,' Lucy snapped at Mum, who was holding a hand to her forehead. 'Ella didn't say anything. That's actually really rude.'

Ella was staring at the floor. 'Perhaps Ella was feeling shy,' Mum said. 'Now who thinks we should have a doughnut in the café?' My mum is very good at changing the subject. If you mention doughnuts, no one in my family can think about anything else.

*

When we finally got home, I watched Chloe stowing her presents away under the bed.

'Do you think Ella hates Greg?' I asked her.

Chloe picked her stuffed gorilla up off the floor and returned him to her pillow. 'Dunno. Ella doesn't normally hate anyone.'

'But she won't talk to him.'

'She doesn't like talking to strangers.'

'I know, but she does do it normally; she says "yes" and "no" and "school is lovely" and all that sort of thing.'

'Maybe she was just in a bad mood. Shall I tell Lucy that I'm only getting her stupid hedgehogs presents if she buys one for Bananas Gorilla? And that he only likes chocolate? Real chocolate, otherwise she'll just draw a bar of chocolate. She did that the year I wanted money.'

But I was still thinking about Ella. It seemed like either she hated Greg or she was just being spectacularly rude, but neither of those things seemed very Ella-ish. I'm not always great at understanding other people's feelings. I thought I knew how Mum felt about the divorce and that she hated Dad, but it turned out that I was mixing up my own feelings in there. I think I sort of expect people to think the same way I do; but not everyone's like me.

I remembered Ella's face in the café. She was obviously unhappy about something. She'd even let Lucy finish her doughnut so there must be something wrong.

I left Chloe attempting to juggle two pillows and Bananas Gorilla and went into Lucy and Ella's bedroom.

Ella was lying on her bed, holding a book, but I don't think she was really reading it.

'Are you worrying about Crystal?' I asked.

'No,' she said.

'Really? You can tell me if you are. Has she been mean to you?'

'No, honestly, she hasn't said anything to me and I'm glad I told her the truth.'

If it wasn't Crystal then it had to be Greg.

'Ella, I've got a problem; I want to help someone, but I don't know how. You're the best person I know at understanding people, apart from Mum, and I can't ask her about this so I need your advice.'

'You want me to advise you?'

'Yep. So there's this girl. This really nice girl who's kind and polite and hard-working. She's totally lovely. Sometimes she's so good that it makes her evil big sister feel a bit queasy, but basically she's nice.'

'*Okaaaaay*,' Ella said slowly.

'But recently this girl has been a bit rude to her mum's new boyfriend.'

'He's not her boyfriend!' Ella said. 'She called him her friend. He's not her boyfriend, is he?'

'Do you mind if he is? Don't you want her to have a boyfriend?'

Ella squirmed with misery. 'It's not that I don't want her to have a nice time.'

'I know. You're always telling her she should go out more.'

Ella scrubbed at her eyes with her fists. 'When I said that, I thought she'd go shopping with Susan or visit the museum with one of the other teachers.'

'Why do you mind if she goes with a man instead? You don't mind about Dad having a girlfriend. You like Suvi.'

'I do like Suvi.' She hesitated. 'But,' she lowered her voice, 'I wasn't sure at first. I've had time to get used to her.'

'Well, you'll get used to whoever Mum picks as a boyfriend. It might not even be this one; she might try lots of different ones.'

Ella looked like she might be sick. 'Do you really think she's going to have loads of different boyfriends? Will they all come round and have coffee? In our house?'

'Why do you care if they visit our house?'

She looked at me and I stared back at her. I was lost again. I could understand that Ella might not like Mum having a boyfriend, I still wasn't super keen myself, but I didn't see what all this business was about our house. It's not as if Ella liked to lie around in her underwear, eating tuna straight from the can like Chloe did.

'I don't know what to say,' I said eventually. 'I'm trying to cheer you up, but I'm not doing a very good job, am I?'

Ella took a deep breath. 'It's hard to explain. If Mum really has to have a boyfriend, I'd rather she did it at a restaurant. Our house is for us.'

'He's not going to move in or anything.'

Ella's eyes widened in horror.

'I just mean that if any of Mum's friends come round they won't be here for long and you're right, it is our home, so we can just carry on doing whatever we want to.'

Ella pressed her lips together.

Then I got it. Ella can't be herself when there are strangers around. 'Do you feel uncomfortable when there are other people in the house?' I asked.

'Sort of. I mean, I don't mind Susan or Lauren, I don't even mind Thunder so much now because he's not as scary as he looks, but . . . when Greg was here, I just sort of froze.'

'It must be difficult for you,' I said.

'I just can't help it. I don't want him to think I'm mean. I'm sure he's very nice.'

'Yes!' I said. 'I bet he is and do you know how I know?'

'How?'

'Because Mum likes him and I think she's a pretty good judge; she wouldn't bring anyone horrible into our house. And you know the way that you got used to Suvi and Thunder? That will happen with Greg too if he keeps coming round.'

'Do you think so?'

'I'm sure of it. You're nice; he's nice. I think eventually you'll get along.'

'But what about now?'

'If you feel shy now, that's OK. We know you're shy. I think even Greg must have realised that. If you just try to say hello and goodbye to him, I promise you that your big-mouthed sisters can fill in all the gaps for you.'

Ella smiled. 'Thank you. I think that would be a big help.'

And the crease between her eyes finally disappeared.

CHAPTER ❤ THIRTY-ONE

'How's the concert coming on?' Lauren asked.

I'd popped round to her house after an extra rehearsal on Monday afternoon.

'Oh, you know, Mr Garcia has reached that point where he looks haunted and sweaty all the time. He kicked off with the usual, "In three days' time, you'll all be onstage."'

Lauren nodded. 'Oh, I know that speech; it's like he's telling you all you've only got a few days left before you're going to be publicly shamed by the worst singing he's ever heard.'

'Yep. Then he moved on to, "Is there any possibility that you might be persuaded to exert the least bit of effort, Ms Strawberry? Mr Tarasewicz?"'

'What did you say? What did Bartek say?'

'He waited till Mr Garcia was finished with us and, when we were walking back to the hall, he jabbed me in the ribs and said, "Miss Strawberry, when are you going to stop flicking your hair and do some nice singing?"'

'He didn't!'

'He did.'

'What did you say?'

'I said, "Stop jabbing me or I won't ask you to Olivia's party."'

Lauren gasped. 'And?'

'He stopped and I asked him to Olivia's party and he said yes.'

'Woooo-hoooo!' Lauren bounced on her bed and I couldn't help laughing.

'So then Mr Garcia came to listen to the group songs and spent the rest of the rehearsal bellowing and stomping and we all had a great time. At least Bartek and I had a great time making silly jokes. I think Mr Garcia might have actually ruptured an internal organ.'

'He'll be all right. He loves it when he's conducting; his little face lights up like ...'

'Like his acrylic jumper has caught fire.'

Lauren snorted with laughter. 'I wish I was at rehearsals,' she said.

'Me too.'

'I can't wait to watch you though. I might make one of those banners like people have at pop concerts.'

'Brilliant. Please can it say, *Amelia Strawberry, you've got the voice of an angel and you have never (regardless of what Mr Garcia might have said) sounded like an enraged walrus?*'

'That's quite a lot to fit on a bit of old sheet. I might just put your face in a heart.'

'Make sure it's a good likeness.'

'Don't worry, monkey faces like yours are my speciality.'

When it was time for me to go, I left Lauren in her bedroom and went downstairs. Mrs Anderson stuck her head out of the sitting room.

'Amelia,' she said in a low voice. 'May I speak to you?' She motioned me into the sitting room. I sat down and crossed my legs neatly. It felt like when the teacher keeps you behind at the end of a lesson. I hoped she wasn't cross with me again. She didn't look it. In fact, she started off with something that was very close to a smile.

'As you know, the last few months have been very difficult for Lauren.'

I nodded hard. 'It's been really tough for her.'

'I'd like to get her something really special for Christmas, but I'm afraid we're rather stumped for ideas. Obviously, she's got her new laptop and she's not had her phone long so I was hoping that perhaps you'd have some idea of what she might like?'

I thought hard. 'I can't think of anything she's mentioned.' Lauren isn't like some people who always have a long list of things that they want. 'Clothes maybe?'

'Perhaps.'

I realised that since Lauren doesn't get to go out so much, clothes might not be the best choice. I wanted to think of something good, but my mind had gone completely blank.

'Well,' she said, 'I mustn't keep you. Perhaps you could think it over and let me know if you come up with anything? Or if Lauren happens to mention something she'd like.'

'Yes, definitely. I can do that.'

And she showed me out. I thought hard about it all the way home. Any kind of jewellery or make-up had the same drawback as clothes: I was sure that Lauren would quite like those things, but they could also be a reminder that she might not get much use out of them. Like her mum said, she didn't need another computer and she was happy with her phone. There must be something that she'd really like. I was going to have to rack my brains.

222

When I got home, Mum was on the phone and I could hear Lucy singing 'Away in a Manger' in the bathroom. I went into the sitting room where Chloe was playing on Mum's laptop.

'What's the best present you've ever had?' I asked her.

'That time Dad got tickets for him and me to watch Man U play Liverpool,' she said without taking her eyes off the screen.

'Hmm.' I didn't think tickets to go anywhere or see anything were a great idea for Lauren because she never knew in advance if she'd be too tired to go.

A wet and completely naked Lucy ran into the middle of the room, dripping bathwater on to the rug. Ella chased after her and managed to throw a bath towel over her. 'Please get dry or you'll freeze,' she begged Lucy.

'What about you, Ella?' I asked. 'What's the best present you've ever had?'

She thought about it. 'When Mum fixed Wellington's fur.'

Ella isn't the type to spoil toys, but unfortunately Lucy is and she managed to spill blackcurrant juice on Ella's teddy a few years ago. I don't know how Mum did it, because Wellington used to belong to my nana so he was very old and fragile, but after she gave Wellington a makeover he looked as good as new.

Lucy didn't wait to be asked, she just announced, 'My best present was Kirsti.'

'Kirsti wasn't a present for you, dummy,' Chloe said.

Lucy shoved Chloe. 'Yes she was. She's my little sister, isn't she? So she's mine.'

'If that's true then she's mine as well, and Ella's and Amelia's.'

Lucy looked at us pityingly. 'I suppose so. But she's only got one favourite and that's me.'

'How do you know?' I asked.

'Because she told me.'

You can't really argue with a seven-year-old who thinks that she can speak to babies so I left it there. Chloe isn't as mature as me so she grabbed Lucy and tried to wrestle her into a full nelson, but Lucy was still slippery and the pair of them ended up rolling around on the rug. Which was quite entertaining, but it wasn't really helping me think of a present for Lauren.

'Stop it!' Ella said and she pulled Lucy away from Chloe and started putting her pyjama top on her. 'You know what's interesting about all those presents?' she asked me while she did up Lucy's buttons.

'What's that?'

'They're not really things, are they? I mean, when you talk about buying a present, you think about something you can find in a shop like a book, or a toy, or a necklace, but the stuff that people really love is something you can't tie a ribbon round.'

I stared at Ella. 'You say some really clever stuff sometimes.'

'Yup, she's a genius,' Chloe said. 'And I am a world-class athlete.' Then she picked up Lucy and dumped her on to the sofa so her feet were on my lap.

'Keep that bare back end away from me!' I said.

Lucy tried to get up, but Chloe pinned her down. 'Get her, Ella!'

And Ella laid in with a tickle. I couldn't help joining in. Lucy shrieked like she was being murdered. We just tickled her more.

Sometimes my sisters are all right.

CHAPTER ✦ THIRTY-TWO

The next morning, I woke up way earlier than usual and I thought about Lauren's present while I was eating breakfast. What Ella had said to me really made sense: some of the best presents are things that happen, not things that you can wrap up.

But it was so hard to think of something that Lauren would want to happen that it was actually possible to carry out. Obviously, what she most wanted, and I wanted for her too, was to get better. But that was out of my hands.

There were lots of places I could think of that Lauren would enjoy going, but it seemed like a bad idea to plan something like that when she might end up not being well enough to go to. That would just make her feel worse. So what did she like? What could she still enjoy? Not much. She was mostly stuck in her room. What if she had a nicer room? Maybe I could offer to paint it. The problem was that Lauren's room wasn't very big.

Then an idea hit me like one of Chloe's punches. What if Lauren moved into her brother's room? It was larger; she'd have room for a desk in there or maybe a comfy chair so that she didn't have to be in bed if she was feeling up to it. It seemed like a brilliant idea. The only problem was that it wasn't my house to rearrange. I didn't feel confident about telling Lauren's parents that they should switch their home about. Surely, if they'd thought that was a good idea, they'd have done it before? And Lauren's brother would be home from uni for the holidays. Would he be cross about losing the big room? I didn't want to start any family fights.

But, the more I thought about it, the more I felt that giving Lauren a nicer room was the most thoughtful present she could have, and I decided I was going to have to suggest it to Lauren's mum, even if she did tell me to mind my own business.

Rather than dropping round, which might make it difficult to get Lauren's mum on her own, I decided it would be best to ring. I picked up the phone straight away in the hope that Lauren might still be in bed.

Mrs Anderson answered after the first ring.

'Hello?'

'Hi ...' I still wasn't quite sure what to call her. 'It's me, Amelia.'

'Hello, Amelia. I'm afraid Lauren's in bed, I usually leave it till a little later to wake her.'

'That's OK. I wanted to speak to you. I've been thinking about Lauren's present.'

'Oh good! Have you thought of something?'

'I did have one idea.'

'What's that?'

'Well, it might not be something you want to do, so don't worry if it's a stupid idea. I just thought that maybe now Matt's gone to university ...'

There was dead silence on the other end of the phone and I nearly lost my nerve.

'... I thought maybe you could give Lauren's room a makeover and perhaps swap her room with Matt's so that she has more space? Maybe for a desk?' I said it all in such a rush that I had to take a big breath when I'd finished.

Lauren's mum didn't say anything.

'It was just a thought. You could get her something completely different.'

'No,' she said slowly. 'No, I think you're on to something. Matthew's room is larger; he needed the space for his rowing machine and his other equipment, but now he's taken all that with him to Leeds we could switch their rooms, couldn't we?'

228

'Yes?'

'We could paint it and get new curtains and bedding. A desk is a good idea for when she's up to schoolwork.'

She definitely seemed to be warming to the idea. 'I thought perhaps a comfy chair,' I said.

'Yes. And the view from the window is nicer too. Oh, there are lots of things we can do – Amelia, it's a brilliant idea!'

I felt my face getting warm. That was possibly the nicest thing she'd ever said to me. 'If you need any help with painting or anything, I could do that.'

'That would be very helpful. I wonder if we might manage to make it a surprise.'

'She'd need to be out of the house for a while if we're going to paint.'

'Lauren's father had planned to take her to her grandmother's for a Christmas visit this weekend. I wonder if we could make that an overnight trip.'

'That would work.'

'Let me think about this. Do you think you could keep this weekend free and I'll get back to you?'

'Definitely.'

'All right then. Thank you so much, Amelia. I think it's a marvellous idea.'

CHAPTER ✿ THIRTY-THREE

When we got to Dad's house the next day, Suvi had put up the Christmas tree, but waited for us so we could decorate it. Which I thought was brave of her given that Suvi likes brown and grey things and Lucy's favourite colour is 'rainbow'.

'Is this all you've got?' Lucy asked, looking at the box of wicker stars and felt birds.

Suvi nodded.

'Don't worry,' Lucy said. 'I made an angel at school. You can have it for your tree.' She beamed at Suvi. 'I used half a tub of glitter on it.'

'Thank you,' Suvi said, and I have to give her credit for completely sounding like she meant it.

Suvi handed Chloe candlesticks for the mantelpiece. 'How's your rugby?' she asked.

'It's brilliant. Coach says I've got great power so now I just need to work on my speed.'

Suvi smiled. 'This is fantastic. So you're getting the same treatment as the boys?'

Chloe's screwed up her face. 'Well, it's not exactly the same as the boys. But I'm sort of trying to forget about that and concentrate on the training.'

Suvi tilted her head to one side. 'You should enjoy what you're doing, yes, but for me, I wouldn't forget about these other things.'

That got Chloe's attention. 'Really? Because the only difference is that they get to play at the stadium. And they got some free stuff. I mean, I do really like free stuff, but, when you think about it, it's only some drinks and a shiny shirt.'

Suvi shook her head. 'When you give something to the boys that's not available to the girls, it's never just a little thing. It's part of a much bigger thing and you should always fight it, right down to the bottles of drinks.'

I hadn't thought about it like that.

'Are you telling Chloe to fight?' Lucy asked with round eyes. 'We're not supposed to fight. Except Chloe does sometimes, and once her and Thunder were fighting and they didn't see the stairs and they rolled all the way down, but it was all right because Chloe landed on Thunder and he's quite like a cushion.'

'I don't mean fighting with fists, I mean fighting with words and actions.'

Lucy's face lit up. She was clearly delighted by the idea of new ways to do battle.

'I'll think about that,' Chloe said and she went back to decorating the mantelpiece.

My phone rang during tea and, even though Suvi scowled a bit, when I told her it was Lauren's home number, she said I should answer it.

'Amelia, it's Lauren's mother. I was wondering if you were still free on Saturday to help with her room?'

'Yes, definitely.'

'Marvellous. Could you come over around ten?'

'OK.'

'I'm going to buy some paint tomorrow. I don't know what your thoughts are, but colour-wise, I was thinking . . .'

'Purple,' we both said together. Lauren is crazy about purple.

'Yes!' she laughed. 'But then I thought purple might be too dark for the actual walls.'

'How about a paler shade? Like lilac?'

'That's a good idea. Then perhaps we could get some purple accessories?'

'Great. I'll see you on Saturday.'

After tea, Chloe and I did the washing-up. At least I did the washing-up while Chloe made us secret sandwiches. No one has ever actually forbidden us from making sandwiches immediately after tea, but I sort of get the idea that Dad might think it looked a bit rude when Suvi has cooked for us. The thing is that I don't mind Suvi's vegetably, grainy cooking that much, but it doesn't always fill me up. So I made lots of splashing noises to cover the sound of Chloe opening the fridge and dropping the cheese on the floor.

'Don't put anything weird in mine,' I whispered. Last time I bit into a sandwich that Chloe had made, I got a mouthful of marmalade and egg. Now I inspect everything she makes for me.

'It's cheese and ham,' Chloe said, putting down a plate next to the sink. 'And here's the ketchup bottle so you can add your own.'

'It's fine as it is, thanks.'

That didn't stop her from adding a large dollop of ketchup to her own sandwich. And a squirt of brown sauce. I looked away as she took a bite and chewed squelchily. 'You know what Suvi said about rugby?' she asked me.

'Mmm–hmm.'

'What do you think? Because Mrs Henderson said that she hoped I wasn't going to continue making a fuss now that I'd got what I wanted.'

'I think that "making a fuss" is what they call it when a girl points out that she ought to be treated equally with the boys.'

Chloe raised her eyebrows. 'You sound like Suvi.'

'I can think of worse people to sound like.'

She swallowed a large bite of sandwich. 'I do understand what Suvi means, but I'm really happy with training. It's what I wanted and I don't know what more I could do, even if I decided that I should do something.'

'Mmm. It's tricky; concentrating on the training seems right, but now Suvi's saying you can't let people treat girls differently just because they're girls, even when it's only a little thing. And that seems right too.'

'Can they both be right?' she asked.

I nodded. 'I suppose so. It depends on the thing that's happening. And it depends on the person. Some people are good at fighting over everything and some people have to ... pick their battles.'

'So what do you think I should do?'

'That's the point. I can't tell you. You have to decide what you think yourself.'

Chloe wiped up a blob of sauce with her finger. 'Urgh. Why does everything have to be so complicated?'

'I don't know. But I think you've done a good job so far.'

'Are you giving me a compliment, Amelia Strawberry? No way!'

'Shut up!' I flicked soapsuds at her. 'Do you want me to call you a hairy-faced baboon to reverse the effects?'

'Nothing can reverse the effects. You said something nice! You love me!'

I sloshed a whole handful of water at her and she squealed and splashed me back.

'What? What is it, girls?' Dad called and we heard the sitting-room door open.

Then we had to shove all the sandwich stuff back in the fridge as quick as we could while we fell about laughing.

CHAPTER ❤ THIRTY–FOUR

On the night of the Christmas concert, I spent longer than usual getting ready. I knew there were going to be a ton of people there and, while the most important thing to me was to sing well, I thought that looking nice couldn't hurt. As the time to leave got nearer, the fluttery feeling in my stomach got worse.

Lauren called me to say good luck. 'Are you still coming?' I asked. I tried not to sound pushy, but I really, really wanted her to be there.

'Of course I am,' she said. 'I can't wait to watch you.'

For once, Mum was super strict about everyone being ready on time. When Lucy tried to dash back into the house for something, she grabbed her round the waist and bundled her into the car. 'Amelia has to be punctual,' she said firmly.

'What did you want anyway?' Ella asked Lucy when we'd got going.

'I need something to read,' Lucy whined.

'It's not a long drive,' Mum said. 'We'll be at Amelia's concert in five minutes.'

'That's what I need the reading for! I've been to Amelia's singing before. It goes on and on and on.'

'Lucy,' Mum said in a warning tone.

'There's probably something to read in the car anyway,' Chloe said. 'Everything else is in here.'

She's right. Our car is extremely messy. The footwells are full of junk: crisp packets, mini juice cartons, apple cores, lost gloves, pens, toys, flip-flops. Chloe swears she saw a mouse once.

Lucy started rummaging through it all and I ran through my song in my head until we arrived at school.

Performers had to go in a different door to the audience so I said goodbye in the car park.

Mum gave me a quick squeeze. 'Your father sent me a text earlier. He should be here any minute. Good luck, sweetheart.'

'You'll be brilliant,' Ella said.

'Yeah, break a leg!' Chloe said.

Lucy's head was buried in *A Guide to British Butterflies*, so I gave up on good wishes from her and walked away on rather wobbly legs.

'Don't forget what I said about farting on stage!' Chloe called.

I pretended I wasn't related to her.

Before I went to what Mr Garcia was calling the green room but was actually Miss Espinoza's Spanish room, I stuck my head in at the back of the hall. The rows of chairs were already filling up. It was loud and crowded and hot. I wondered if I could get someone to open some windows; when Lauren gets hot, it makes her feel worse.

In fact, the whole set-up wasn't exactly ideal for her. The chairs were hard and the concert was going to last for hours. I remembered the last time Lauren had a late night; she'd slept in the next day until lunchtime. If she came tonight, I wondered if she'd make it in to school tomorrow for the last day of term. The last day is always really good fun. Lauren was particularly looking forward to it because Mrs Holt had put us in a team with Cute Josh for an end-of-term quiz.

For a moment, I was frozen with indecision. I really wanted Lauren to come. But then I realised that I really wanted things to be the best they could be for her. And I knew that meant choosing school tomorrow with Christmas presents and cards from her friends, and chocolates from the teachers, and doing the quiz with Josh. Not the long, hot crush of tonight. So I called her.

'What do you mean you don't want me to

come?' she asked. 'I was just about to leave.'

'It's not that I don't want you to, but it's a late night. I'm not on till near the end. It's going to tire you out, isn't it?'

'Maybe, but I don't mind; it'll be worth it.'

'I don't want you to miss tomorrow.'

She was quiet for a moment. 'I don't mind,' she said again. She'd obviously already realised that tonight might take its toll and I was really touched that she'd decided she was prepared to miss the last day of term to see me sing. But I wasn't going to let her make that sacrifice.

'My mind is made up,' I said. 'I need you here tomorrow so you'd better get your sleep tonight. Don't worry, I'll get Dad to film me singing because obviously you won't want to miss it completely.'

She laughed. 'Obviously. But are you sure you're OK with me not being there?'

'I'll miss you, but this way we get the last day of term together. And look on the bright side: once it's on film, you'll be able to watch me performing over and over again.'

'Fantastic.'

When that was done, I sent a text to my dad to make sure he videoed me singing. Then I sent another text to Suvi to get her to make sure my dad looked at his messages.

Inside the green room, everyone was getting excited. There was a lot of giggling and people flapping about when they didn't really need to be flapping about.

I raised an eyebrow at Bartek to show that I thought they were all being childish, but I've got to admit that my insides were flapping about a bit themselves. I hoped I'd feel a bit less sick once I'd got onstage.

Mr Garcia came in and glared at us. He looked awful. There were rings around his eyes, his skin looked waxy and when he said, 'Quiet, please,' his voice broke. I thought he was going to give us a lecture, but he clearly wasn't up to it because he just took us through a quick warm-up and finished with, 'Let's get this over with.'

Fortunately, Mr O'Brien obviously felt a lot less doomed about the whole thing. He beamed at us and said, 'This is it! Have fun!' And led us out onstage.

The audience fell silent. We shuffled into our positions and Mr Garcia counted us in for 'Walking in a Winter Wonderland'. The audience seemed to really enjoy it; Mr O'Brien was right about getting people in the mood with something they know.

The more we sang, the more the audience seemed to warm up. Some of them were even swaying and mouthing along with the words. I looked out into the hall for my family. I spotted Lucy first; she was reading a road map. She was sitting with Mum on one side and Chloe on the other. Dad was next, then Suvi with Kirsti on her lap. But on the other side of Mum was a gap. Where Lauren should have been. It did give me a little pang. But I'd realised that Lauren was going to have to make decisions about what she could do and what was the best way to use her limited energy. She wasn't going to be able to be there at all the places I would like her to. But I knew that she *wanted* to be with me. And that's how things were. It wasn't perfect, but it was enough.

Finally, it was time for my duet with Bartek.

I stepped out of my row and moved up to the front spot. My legs managed to get me all the way there without buckling.

I looked at Bartek; as always, he was grinning away at me. I tried to smile back, but my lips stuck to my teeth so it was probably more like a werewolf snarl, but there was no time to think about that because Mr Garcia was counting the orchestra in and I needed to concentrate.

I took one last look at my smiling family, then I focused back on Mr Garcia's conducting hand, took a deep breath and started to sing.

CHAPTER ❤ THIRTY-FIVE

'*AHHHHHH!*' Lauren shrieked at me when I came into our tutor room the next morning. 'You were amazing!'

I laughed.

'Fabulous!' She squeezed me into a hug. 'I fell asleep before your dad sent me the video, but I have watched it three times already this morning. I might fit in another viewing before English.'

'Well,' I said, freeing myself from her crushing embrace, 'when you watch me and Bartek, you are probably seeing the best bit. Really, you've got to feel sorry for the poor people who had to sit through all that other nonsense.'

'Hmm,' she said. 'Talent and modesty.'

'I thought you said I was good!'

'You were, but aren't you supposed to blush and

tell me I'm too kind when I give you compliments?'

I laid a hand on her arm in mock seriousness. 'Lauren, I'm very sorry to tell you that if that's the kind of girl you're looking for, you've got the wrong Amelia.'

We cracked up.

It was a brilliant day. None of the teachers tried to make us do any work. Instead, we played games and watched videos.

All day long, I kept sneaking looks at Lauren and wondering what she'd say when she saw her new bedroom.

After lunch, I walked her to the car park.

'You know my dad's taking me to my grandma's tomorrow, don't you?' she asked. 'But how about coming over on Sunday afternoon?'

I almost let out a laugh because I knew that I'd be at her house before that, but I nodded instead. 'Sure, see you then.'

And she climbed into her mum's car. It's a good job Lauren didn't look back at me because, as they drove off, I swear Mrs Anderson winked at me, and then I really did start laughing.

In the morning, as soon as Lauren and her dad were safely in the car, Mrs Anderson sent me a text and I walked round to Lauren's house.

'Hello, Amelia,' Mrs Anderson said when she opened the door. 'Thank you so much for coming.' She led me up the stairs. 'We've got some extra help because Matthew arrived back yesterday, so we've already got started.'

They'd done more than that: they'd moved every single thing out of his room.

'Right!' Lauren's mum said. 'I'll fetch the paint from the garage.' And she left me alone with Matt.

'How's it going, Amelia?' he asked.

'Fine, thanks. Hope you don't mind about your room.' I felt sort of responsible that he was losing his bedroom.

'Nah, I'm hardly here. And it'll be really nice for Loz.'

Mrs Anderson came back and we got going. Last time we painted a room in our house, Mum just threw some sheets over things and we got on with it, but Lauren's mum was much more methodical. We carefully covered the carpet and put masking tape on the skirting boards and the picture rail. Once we actually began painting, it went pretty quickly.

'That's gone on well, hasn't it?' Lauren's mum said while we were having a break and a cup of tea. 'Now I think we'll leave Matthew to finish the fiddly bits and we'll pop to the shops.'

So we got in the car and drove to one of those big out-of-town home stores. We chose a purple rug, a purple lamp and a sort of patchwork-effect duvet cover in purple and lilac, with matching curtains. When we got back, Mrs Anderson showed me the desk that Lauren's dad had already assembled in the garage and I helped her carry it up the stairs and place it in the middle of Lauren's new room, along with everything else.

'It's quick-drying paint,' Lauren's mum said, 'but I think I'll wait till tomorrow morning to move everything into place.' She sighed happily. 'Thank you so much, Amelia, and you are coming round tomorrow to see Lauren's face, aren't you? I could ask Lauren and her dad to pick you up on their way back from Lauren's grandmother's.'

'That would be great,' I said. 'Thanks . . .' I hesitated for a second, 'Mrs Anderson.'

'Oh, do call me Kate,' she said.

And, for the first time since I'd met her, I thought I might actually be able to do that.

CHAPTER ❤ THIRTY-SIX

When I climbed into the back seat of Mr Anderson's car the next day, it was obvious that Lauren didn't have a clue that there was something going on. She started telling me all about her shopping trip with her grandma and about the scarf that she'd bought for her mum.

When we got to the house, Mrs Anderson, I mean *Kate*, opened the door before we'd even got out of the car. Matt was hovering behind her. They were both grinning.

'What's happening?' Lauren asked.

'We've got something to show you,' Lauren's dad said.

Lauren looked at me with raised eyebrows. I couldn't help giggling.

'You're in on this too!' Lauren said. She was

clearly confused by the idea of me and her family having a joint secret.

'What is it?' she asked.

'Come upstairs!' Lauren's mum led the way. Her face was glowing like a little kid's does when they've got something exciting to tell you.

We stopped outside Lauren's new room.

Lauren nudged me. 'What's going on?'

'Close your eyes,' I said.

'What are you lot up to?' she asked, but she closed her eyes anyway.

Her mum opened the door and said, 'Surprise!'

Lauren opened her eyes.

For a moment, she just stared. So did I; the room looked completely different now everything was in place.

'No way!' Lauren squealed. 'Is this for me?'

'Of course!' her dad said. 'Come in and take a proper look!'

I followed Lauren into the room. The pale lilac walls we'd chosen looked calm and light. There was the desk under the window with Lauren's laptop and school books and the purple lamp on top of it. Lauren's old bookshelf was still crammed with her favourite books, but there were three new photo frames sitting on it. The top of her chest of drawers was arranged like a dressing table with a standing mirror, and her bottles of perfume and make-up grouped around it. It all looked amazing, but the biggest surprise was that on the opposite wall to Lauren's bed, instead of a comfy chair like I'd suggested, there was a sort of sofa thing. Kate hadn't shown me that the day before.

She followed my line of sight. 'This . . .' she said, laying a hand on one of the cushions of the sofa thing, 'is a daybed; you two can sit on it during the daytime and, when Lauren is up to it, Amelia can stay the night.'

Lauren looked at me and yelped. 'I can't believe it!' She threw her arms round her mum and dad and Matt. 'Thank you! Thank you so much. This is the best room ever!'

Her dad put his hands up. 'My contribution was mostly getting you out of the way.'

Kate's cheeks were flushed. 'And I had some help with the decorating. Your brother did a lot of painting and as for Amelia . . .' She turned to look at me. 'Without her, this wouldn't have happened. It was all her idea.'

Lauren hugged me too. 'Thank you as well! You're all brilliant.'

*

Later on, after we'd checked out all the cool new things in the room, Lauren's family went downstairs and the two of us lay side by side on the daybed, trying it out for size.

'Do you think you'll be able to stay over one night next week?' Lauren asked.

'Of course. I'll bring the chocolate.'

Lauren gave a contented sigh. 'You know what? For a while, I was so panicked about this whole CFS thing. I kept looking up stuff online and freaking out whenever I read that some people take years to recover, but now I feel more positive. I might be lucky, it might go away, or I might not even have it at all; the doctor says it's hard to be definite and this could all still be the after-effects of glandular fever. I figure I might as well be optimistic.'

She certainly sounded a lot brighter about it.

'That's a good attitude to take,' I said.

'And if it is going to be a problem for a long time ...' Her voice wobbled just a tiny bit. 'If it is then I'll just have to get through it. Even when things are bad, there's always this.' She squeezed my hand and I knew that she meant us two just hanging out together.

'Yep,' I said.

When I was little, I thought that being friends was only about having fun. Then I realised that there's a bit more to it, and that your friends need your love and support. In the last few weeks, I've had to work out that sometimes it can be difficult to give that love and support, but it's worth it. Because all that caring and putting the other person's needs first is like a gift that you can give to your friend and it's better than chocolates or jewellery, it's even better than a new bedroom, because it really shows how much you love them. I squeezed Lauren's hand back.

'Do you know something?' I said. 'Even though you're always telling me I smell and pulling that horrible face you do, there is actually nothing you can do to get rid of me. I will absolutely always be here.'

'Good,' she said. 'Because I need my friends. And I need you especially, Amelia.'

Then she forgot she was already on the edge of the bed and tried to roll over. Instead, she landed in a heap on the floor.

We cracked up.

Can't get enough of the
STRAWBERRY SISTERS?

Want to know how to bake Chloe's banana
bread? Or which STRAWBERRY SISTER
you're most like when it comes
to friendship?

Then turn the page for some fun extras!

STRAWBERRY SISTERS PROFILES

AMELIA
Age: 13

 Hobbies: singing about sad things, painting her nails black and being sarcastic

Favourite food: pizza

Favourite phrase: 'That's a stupid idea'

Dream job: singer in a band

CHLOE
Age: 12

Hobbies: wrestling, hockey, rugby (if you can knock your teeth out doing it, Chloe loves it)

Favourite food: curry, chocolate and cake (sometimes all at the same time)

Favourite phrase: 'Can I have some more?'

Dream job: crisp taster

ELLA
Age: 11

🍓 Hobbies: making films with Ashandra and karaoke with Kayleigh

🍓 Favourite food: brownies

🍓 Favourite phrase: 'I'll do it'

🍓 Dream job: working with numbers and nice people

LUCY
Age: 7

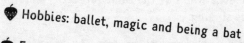

🍓 Hobbies: ballet, magic and being a bat

🍓 Favourite food: spaghetti with tomato ketchup

🍓 Favourite phrase: 'NO!'

🍓 Dream job: magician or Bat Queen

KIRSTI
Age: 0

🍓 Hobbies: dribbling, sleeping and gurgling

🍓 Favourite food: milk

🍓 Favourite phrase: 'Waaaaaaaaah!'

🍓 Dream job: cot tester

STRAWBERRY SISTERS QUIZ: WHAT KIND OF FRIEND ARE YOU?

WHAT DO YOU LIKE DOING WITH YOUR FRIENDS?
a) I'm fine doing whatever they want to do.
b) Sport. Mud. Food. That's all you need for a good time.
c) I don't mind what we play, as long as I get to choose and everybody does what I say.
d) Going shopping, talking about cute boys, laughing at how ridiculous our teachers are.

WHAT QUALITIES DO YOU LOOK FOR IN A BEST FRIEND?
a) Someone who's nice to other people.
b) Great ball skills and a powerful right hook.
c) Generosity. So they can give all their good stuff to me.
d) Someone who has the same sarcastic sense of humour and likes singing.

HOW DO YOU FEEL IF YOU HAVEN'T SEEN YOUR BEST FRIEND IN A WHILE?
a) A bit sad but sometimes people are busy and as long as they're okay I don't mind.
b) Not great, have you ever tried wrestling on your own?
c) Unless I need someone to be my horse / slave / armchair I wouldn't even notice.
d) Awful and a bit mad if I'm honest, but only because I feel totally lost without them.

WHAT DO YOU DO IF YOUR BEST FRIEND FORGETS SOMETHING REALLY IMPORTANT TO YOU?
a) I'd be sad but I'm sure they'd never do anything like that on purpose.
b) Tell everyone apart from my friend how rubbish it is.
c) Plot my revenge.
d) I'd be devastated - but my best friend is so cool that I know she wouldn't do that.

TWO OF YOUR FRIENDS HAVE AN ARGUMENT, WHOSE SIDE DO YOU TAKE?

a) No one's! I'd want them to talk and make up. I really hate it when people argue.

b) I'd get them to have a wrestling match and go with whoever wins.

c) Whoever gives me the most sweets.

d) If it involved my very best friend I'd take her side, of course! It doesn't matter if she's the one who's really in the wrong.

YOUR FRIEND TELLS YOU SOME JUICY GOSSIP. DO YOU TELL ANYONE?

a) Of course not! I don't like it when people say mean things about other people behind their backs, it's horrible.

b) If it's about boyfriends, it's too boring to pass on. But if someone farted in geography, I'll tell everyone.

c) It depends. What will you give me if I keep quiet?

d) If my best friend told me something I'd never betray her confidence. Maybe if someone else told me something interesting.

HOW DO YOU SHOW YOUR FRIENDS YOU CARE ABOUT THEM?

a) By being nice of course.

b) With a really good rugby tackle.

c) They should be showing how much they care about ME.

d) Teasing them, sharing silly jokes and chocolate.

HOW DO YOU SAY THANK YOU TO YOUR FRIENDS?

a) Say thank you, of course! Manners are really important.

b) A marmalade and chutney sandwich. Or a friendly arm punch.

c) They should be saying thank you to ME.

d) I'd say thanks but I'd throw a sarcastic remark in too. My friends really get my sense of humour.

YOUR BEST FRIEND HASN'T DONE SO WELL IN A TEST AT SCHOOL.
DO YOU . . .
a) Comfort them and offer to help them revise for next time.
b) Remind them of the things they are good at.
c) Tell them how well you did.
d) Give them a hug. Then tell them about the time you didn't do so great, hopefully you can both laugh about it together.

WHY ARE FRIENDS IMPORTANT?
a) Because everyone needs friends.
b) There are loads of sports that you need a partner for.
c) Sometimes I have jobs that need doing.
d) It's nice to have someone you can talk to about things.

TURN THE PAGE FOR THE ANSWERS . . .

MOSTLY 'A'S

You're a friend like Ella! You're sweet by nature and manners are very important to you. And because you're always peppy and kind, your friends always feel special and you're the first person they come to when they need advice. Though you always put others first and hate to argue, sometimes you need to be more assertive and tell people how you feel. It'll make you even happier in the long run and your true friends will respect you for it.

MOSTLY 'B'S

You're a friend like Chloe! You're a whirlwind of energy and happiest when you and your friends are something active together. Although you're quite boisterous you find it hard to talk to your friends when you're upset and find it easier to complain to your family rather than face friendship problems head on. You need to realise that relationships are about balance: good and bad. A real friend will want to help you when you feel sad and fix things, so be honest. Your friendships will be even stronger because of it.

MOSTLY 'C'S

You're a friend like Lucy! You feel very comfortable in telling people what to do so you're a natural leader in your group of friends, although you can act like your needs are more important than anyone else's around you. At times this can be too much and people don't always respond in the way you want them to. Sometimes you have to pull back and let others enjoy attention and remember that you're not the most important person in the group. The more you help, support and share with your friends the more they'll appreciate all your good qualities.

MOSTLY 'D'S

You're a friend like Amelia! You'd be lost without your best friend because you do everything together and you pride yourself in being the very best BFF. Sometimes you get a little wrapped up in your own problems and you need to check that others are okay too. You also tend to shut others out in favour of your bestie, so try to remember that while it's great having a BFF, it's okay to have other friends too. Your loyalty is clear though and it's one of your best qualities; if only everyone could be lucky enough to have a BFF like you.

BANANA BREAD RECIPE BY CHLOE

Remember when I pummelled a load of bananas because I was mad that I didn't get on to the rugby squad? Suvi doesn't like food to get wasted so we made something delicious with my banana victims.

Here's the recipe for you to try. Make sure you've got a grown up around to help (and to tell you where they've hidden the sugar).

INGREDIENTS
200G PLAIN FLOUR
200G CASTER SUGAR
50G SOFTENED BUTTER
1 TEASPOON VANILLA EXTRACT
1 TEASPOON BICARBONATE OF SODA
1/2 TEASPOON BAKING POWDER
1 EGG
3 VERY RIPE BANANAS

METHOD
Get your adult to preheat oven to 180 C / Gas 4. Then grease and flour a 13x23cm loaf tin. That means ripping off a little bit of the butter wrapper and using it to rub a blob of butter around the tin. When you've finished you can stick the bit of paper in your sister's hair (but she will scream like an angry warthog).

Mash the bananas up (you don't have to pretend that it's anyone's face that you're squashing, but sometimes it makes you feel better if you do) and then add the measured out flour, sugar, butter, vanilla, baking powder, bicarbonate of soda and egg.

Give everything a really good mix.

Pour into loaf tin. When you slop the mixture out, it's all lumpy and banana-y and it reminded me of monkey sick, but don't worry, it looks much better when it's cooked.

Bake at 180 C / Gas 4 for 50 to 60 minutes or until skewer inserted into centre of loaf comes out clean.

Eat loads! I told Suvi that eating fruit is important to your health and that I needed at least three slices.

Just like Ella, Candy Harper grew up in a rather small house with a rather large family. As the fourth of five sisters it was often hard to get a word in edgeways, so she started writing down her best ideas. It's probably not a coincidence that her first 'book' featured an orphan living in a deserted castle.

Growing up, she attended six different schools, but that honestly had very little to do with an early interest in explosives.

Candy has been a bookseller, a teacher and the person who puts those little stickers on apples. She is married and has a daughter named after Philip Pullman's Lyra.

You can follow her on Twitter @CandyHarper_